"When Something Catches My Attention, I Want to Know Everything About It,"

Nicholas said, looking directly at her, his dark eyes intense. Suddenly the night seemed filled with anticipation.

Thea looked away, afraid that her emotions showed too clearly on her face. She warned herself silently that this was a man who would be difficult to control, perhaps impossible.

"Goddesses aren't supposed to be afraid of mere mortals," murmured Nicholas softly, a light, teasing quality to his voice. "Why are you so cautious?"

She met his eyes unflinchingly. "You're a very attractive man," she whispered. "On an island like this, with a man like you, it would be easy to forget to be careful."

BETSY McCARTY

wanted to be a writer from the time she was six. She just got sidetracked for twenty years. After working as a history teacher, submarine planner, and an electrical components buyer, she finally returned to her first love—writing. She now lives in the resort town of Saratoga Springs, New York, and devotes herself full time to her "fictional friends."

Dear Reader:

I'd like to take this opportunity to thank you for all your support and encouragement of Silhouette Romances.

Many of you write in regularly, telling us what you like best about Silhouette, which authors are your favorites. This is a tremendous help to us as we strive to publish the best contemporary romances possible.

All the romances from Silhouette Books are for you, so enjoy this book and the many stories to come.

Karen Solem
Editor-in-Chief
Silhouette Books

BETSY McCARTY
The Golden Rose

Silhouette *Romance*

Published by Silhouette Books New York

America's Publisher of Contemporary Romance

SILHOUETTE BOOKS, a Division of Simon & Schuster, Inc.
1230 Avenue of the Americas, New York, N.Y. 10020

Distributed by Pocket Books

ISBN: 0-671-57332-2

First Silhouette Books printing November, 1984

10 9 8 7 6 5 4 3 2 1

Map by Ray Lundgren

America's Publisher of Contemporary Romance

Printed in the U.S.A.

To Lula—who showed me
the magic in books . . . Thank you

The Golden Rose

GREECE

Places in *italics* are fictitious.

Chapter One

Thea Hunt peered once more from the window of the giant 747, marveling again at the brilliant glory of the world seen at twenty-eight thousand feet. The sunlight blazed golden on the white clouds below. She studied them briefly and then glanced beyond to the horizon where the endless sky blended with the blue of the vast Atlantic. It was exhilarating to soar through the air, and she loved every minute of it.

Since traveling was both her business and her hobby, Thea felt completely at home in the huge plane. She stretched out comfortably, glad that the seats of the 747 were more than ample for her tall slender frame. Flight 942 had only been in the air four hours. It would be some time before she reached her destination, the island of Melinas in the waters off western Greece. She sat back in her seat, unaware that the sunlight had turned her copper-colored hair to a flaming gold and the turquoise of her eyes to a brighter blue than usual. Her thoughts were riveted on the trip ahead of her.

She recalculated the flight schedule, factoring in the

time changes involved in intercontinental travel. It took her a moment, but she was used to figuring numbers quickly, and soon she arrived at their landing time in Greece. It would be four in the afternoon in Athens.

Absently smoothing a wrinkle in her white linen skirt, Thea reviewed her itinerary again and frowned. Arrival in Athens at four and departure by small plane for Melinas at six. That gave her just two hours to get her luggage, go through customs, and find the terminal for the local airline which flew the island traffic. And she had to catch that plane. It was the only flight to Melinas each day.

Melinas. Thea smiled to herself. She could scarcely believe that she was finally on her way to that magical island in the Ionian Sea. Since she was a little girl she had heard tales of the ancient island from her grandmother Helene, whom Thea had called Yaya, the Greek word for grandmother. Helene Louris had been born in Melinas and had spent her girlhood among the ancient ruins that covered the sunny, hot island. But when she was eighteen she had married John Melos, and the young couple had emigrated to America to live in New York City.

Their daughter, Sofia, had had no curiosity about Greece. Totally rooted in New York, she had taken little interest in her mother's tales. It was Thea who loved to sit on Helene Melos' knee after Sunday dinner and listen to stories about Melinas. Drawing from her happy memories, Yaya had painted a wonderful picture for her granddaughter, making the island more and more real for Thea. Thea felt that she knew what the Ionian Sea looked like, and the prancing baby lambs, and the orange trees heavy with fruit.

Best of all for Thea were Yaya's tales of the ancient gods and goddesses whose activities had thrilled people for over two thousand years. Instead of daydreaming about characters from *Grimm's Fairy Tales,* Thea had fantasized about Apollo, the sun god, and the wood nymphs and naiads that populated the earth like fairies. With each passing year, Thea's determination to visit Melinas had become stronger.

Each story session would end the same way. "Someday," Thea would say, "I'm going to go there. We'll go together, Yaya."

"Of course, darling, of course. And we'll visit my old house, and I'll show you my island." Yaya would smile at the thought of visiting her old home. Thea's eyes filled now with tears, and her throat ached. Yaya had died quietly in her sleep almost three years ago, without ever having returned to the warm, sunny land of her youth.

But Thea was going. She glanced down at the white leather shoulder bag containing the letter from her cousin Aletha. Ten years ago the two girls had started corresponding, writing to each other in English, which Aletha was learning from the village priest in Melinas. Thea had just turned sixteen.

Impulsively, Thea reached into her bag and removed the envelope from Aletha. Even though she had almost memorized the letter, she wanted to read it again.

Dear Thea,

This short note is to inform you that the land once owned by Grandmother Louris' family is going to be sold. It consists of approximately one acre of land with its own private beach. Also on the property is a small stucco house built before the turn of the century. As you know, this is the house in which your grandmother was born. There are two bedrooms, a kitchen, and a large living room facing the sea. The present owners have added a small but adequate bath.

Anyway, I wished to inform you, since your dream was to buy a vacation retreat on Melinas. The owners are asking the equivalent of twenty thousand American dollars.

I hope you are well, and also your mother and father. My husband, Dimitri, is well, and so is

the rest of the family. Let me know what you think
about the land.

Love,
Aletha

Did she want the land? More than anything in the
world! Thea folded the letter and put it carefully back
into her purse. Settling back in her seat, she wondered
at the strange series of events leading up to this day.
Sometimes dreams came true in the most unexpected
ways.

She frowned, and again glanced out the window of
the plane. This time, however, she didn't concentrate
on the play of sunlight on the clouds. Instead, her
thoughts flew back to New York, and to the small
business she and her friend Carla had made into a
success. The Magnificent Mermaid was a shop specia-
lizing in materials imported from all over the world,
especially from the Caribbean islands and Mexico. It
was Thea's baby, her pride and joy.

She and Carla had been roommates in college. Both
had been business majors, but neither had any desire
to join a large corporation. During senior year they
had spent their spring break in Jamaica, and both
were delighted by the local handicrafts. Could they
sell these exotic products in Manhattan? They spent
the rest of their senior year discussing just such a
business venture, and after graduation they decided to
go ahead with the idea. Carla's father had co-signed a
loan, and Thea and Carla established their shop.

Both women loved the work. Carla managed the
business end, while Thea concentrated on studying
the buying trends of the public and doing the actual
purchasing, either from a middleman or by traveling
to the islands herself. Her taste was excellent, and she
filled the shop with wonderful buys of native jewelry,
brightly woven baskets, and colorful rugs and clothes.

The Magnificent Mermaid's first year was difficult.
But soon the little business on the Upper East Side of
Manhattan became known, and the third year saw

them pay off their loan in full and start making a decent profit. The last two years had been even more successful.

To Thea life was nearly perfect. She loved her career, especially the traveling. Exotic places had always held a fascination for her, and now she traveled as part of her work: Mexico, Aruba, the Bahamas, Jamaica and the small countries of Central America were all part of her itinerary. One week she would be in New York, the next on Martinique shopping for merchandise. The demands of her job continually led her in new and exciting directions.

Thea's only problem was that work took up all her time, leaving her no room for establishing a relationship with a man. During college she had dated casually, but she had never fallen in love. And the years right after school had been too filled with work to allow her to meet anyone. Her parents and friends would subtly hint that it was time to find the right man, but Thea had laughed away their fears. She was young and successful. When fate decreed, the right man would come along.

It had seemed that she was right. She had met Robert, a successful lawyer from Manhattan, on a business trip to Jamaica. They continued to date in New York, and their friendship turned slowly and, Thea thought, rather methodically into a "relationship."

Everything Robert did, he did methodically, even make love to her. She was a virgin, and intended to remain one until her wedding night. But even with her inexperience she found his gentle kisses and caresses lukewarm. Since she had nothing to compare them with, she told herself that she was satisfied, though she did wonder where those romance writers got all the "passion and excitement" that filled their books. When Robert gave her a diamond for Christmas she had been content if not elated.

The contentment had lasted about two weeks. Robert, Thea discovered belatedly, had extremely definite ideas about the role of a wife and they were patterned sometime prior to World War I. According to Robert a wife cooked all meals from scratch, listened attentively to her husband's problems, did only a minimum of work outside the home, and never traveled without her husband.

It then took Thea only a short while to realize that she did not want to be a wife, or at least not Robert Graham's wife. Quickly and kindly, she returned his ring.

Thea smiled now. It was strange how things worked out. The money she had saved for the house she'd planned to share with Robert was now enough to purchase the land in Greece. Perhaps it was meant to be. She had wanted to own land on Melinas since the time she first heard Yaya Helene's tales. On Melinas she would find her roots, her history. Her father's people, good Scots-Irish Americans, had been in the United States for over two hundred years. Melinas offered her a more exotic past.

She had planned it all out carefully. With Carla's enthusiastic agreement they decided to expand the merchandise in the store to include more items from the Mediterranean countries. Thea would make two buying trips to Greece each year, and combine business with vacations on Melinas. The rest of the time she would rent out the house on a monthly basis, using Aletha as her agent. With all the tourists visiting the Greek Islands, the plan was bound to be profitable.

A slight stirring from under the blanket in the next seat brought her out of her reverie. She glanced at her seat mate, a young man of about twenty who had fallen asleep right after takeoff and had not stirred since. Now he peered over at her, his blue eyes twinkling and his freckled face twisting up in a smile.

"Guess I've been out like the proverbial light," he said sheepishly. "A little too much celebration before the trip."

"Don't worry. I would have wakened you if there had been a problem," said Thea, smiling. "I usually sleep on long flights myself. I was just restless today."

"Actually, this is my first flight. By the way, my name's Mike Robins," he said introducing himself.

"Thea Hunt. You've picked a great day to fly for the first time. There's barely a cloud in the sky now. You can actually see the ocean, and we're about five miles up."

"Really?" Mike leaned over her, straining to see.

Amused, Thea quickly spoke. "Hey, listen. Why don't we trade seats? I've been looking for a while and I'm ready to read my book."

"Sure you don't mind?" Mike asked eagerly.

"Not at all."

They made the change, and Thea settled down in the aisle seat and opened her book, a romance set in ancient Greece. Within minutes she was lost in the plot.

She didn't know what made her look up some time later. Perhaps it was some movement out of the corner of her eye. One moment she was in ancient Greece, reading about a handsome king, and the next moment she thought she saw him walking down the aisle of the 747. It was as if the fantasy hero from her novel had suddenly come to life in the flesh and blood man now approaching her. Two words flashed through her mind—Greek god!

To be sure, the expensive light gray silk suit and pearl white shirt placed this man firmly in the twentieth century, but the intense masculine aura surrounding him was timeless. He had paused in his walk to allow the stewardess to assist a passenger, and Thea had time to observe him carefully. Mentally she compared his physical characteristics with those of the mythical king.

Both men were tall, with wavy black hair and dark eyes, and each conveyed a silent strength and authority. But there the resemblance ended. Whereas the mythical king was described as having the bulky strength of Hercules, the man facing Thea was muscular in a more sinewy way, reminding her of a panther ready to spring. His complexion was dark, and his skin deeply tanned. For one moment she wondered whether he was Greek or Italian. Then she quickly discarded the notion. There was a quality about him, an air of freedom perhaps, which unmistakably marked him as an American.

Feeling her eyes upon him, he turned to face her, and before she could turn away she realized that he had seen her studying him. When their eyes met, Thea felt something akin to a jolt of recognition. She felt as if she knew him, yet she was positive that she had never laid eyes on him before! She definitely would have remembered this man!

He smiled slightly, appraising her high, small breasts and slim waist. His glance hesitated for an instant on her legs, and she realized that her white linen skirt had ridden up, exposing her sun-tanned thigh. To her surprise, she felt herself flush warmly as she straightened her skirt.

Annoyed at her reaction to him, but trying to hide it, Thea acknowledged his smile. She hoped that she looked poised and sophisticated, but with irritation she saw the "Greek god's" black eyes light up with amusement.

Now thoroughly disgusted with herself, Thea forced her eyes back down to her book. At that moment the stewardess moved, and the man walked by. As he passed, Thea caught the scent of a subtle cologne that made her think of salt wind and the sea. The scent intrigued her, and it took all of her willpower not to turn and look behind her.

It was another few hours before they landed in Paris, but Thea found her thoughts wandering from the fictional hero of her book to the real-life "hero" who sat somewhere behind her. He was the best-looking man she had ever seen. When he didn't disembark during the stopover in Paris, she realized that he was bound for Athens, too. Irrationally, the discovery was both disturbing and exciting.

But when the 747 soared into the sky and turned south toward Greece, Thea forgot the dark stranger as she became lost in the excitement of anticipation. Soon she would reach Greece, a magical land so different from the world she had known all her life. The seed for this trip had been planted when she was a child. Today was the culmination of that dream.

It was only two hours from Paris to Athens, but it seemed like forever to Thea. Restlessly she reviewed her schedule yet again and was relieved to hear the pilot say that they would be arriving on time at four o'clock sharp. In Paris she and Mike had returned to their original seats, so now she eagerly scanned the sky for signs of Athens. They were only minutes from the capital when the captain announced that they were approaching the airport and would soon be able to glimpse the Acropolis, the landmark that held the remains of temples and altars sacred to the ancient Greeks.

Thea strained in her seat, holding her breath as the outskirts of the city came into view. For one moment she was disappointed. Athens looked no different from any other large metropolis. But then, perched on top of a craggy hill, she saw a temple gleaming in the sunlight, its marble columns reflecting a golden light like an ancient beacon welcoming her home. Greece! She was here at last!

It took almost half an hour to unload all the passengers from the huge plane, and then another half hour to pick up her luggage. As Thea carried her suitcase and shoulder bag toward customs, she glanced anxiously at her watch. It was almost five. Her flight to Melinas left at six. It was going to be close.

There were several people ahead of her in the customs line, and her nervousness increased as the line moved with Mediterranean slowness. By the time her turn came up, the clock read five-thirty, and it was almost twenty to six when she started for the distant hangar that served as a terminal for Ionian Airways.

Damn, why do I always overpack? she thought as the weight of her suitcase slowed her down. The corridor leading from the main terminal suddenly seemed impossibly long. She stopped to readjust her shoulder bag, and jumped when a deep, masculine voice with a slight Boston accent spoke directly behind her.

"Need some help?" the voice queried. "I'll be glad to carry that suitcase for you."

Thea spun around, amazed to find the "Greek god" from the plane staring down at her, wincing slightly in pain. She had turned so quickly that her suitcase had struck his thigh.

"I'm sorry. Did I hurt you?" she asked hastily, flushing at her own clumsiness. Of all the men in the world she could have bruised, she had to pick this one!

"I'll live, don't worry," he said smiling, revealing straight white teeth. "I startled you. I'm sorry."

Thea looked up at him, trying not to stare. Up close he was even more handsome, though there was a rugged quality to his features that she had failed to recognize earlier. Now she could see the faint lines at the corners of his eyes, which she decided were from sun and wind more than age. He looked about thirty-five.

She gave her head a little shake, trying to bring herself back down to earth. "I was hurrying to catch a plane, and I'm still running late. You'll have to excuse me."

Those lines at his eyes which she had been studying now crinkled up in a smile, and he spoke again. "Why don't you let me carry that monstrous piece of luggage. You must be moving permanently to Greece."

Thea grinned. "Actually, I'm only staying two weeks. I always overpack. It's one of my vices." She had meant to be flippant, but to her horror she saw the stranger raise one dark eyebrow in question, and for an instant she thought he was going to ask her what other vices she had.

But instead, he just picked up her suitcase and began to walk down the corridor. "Hurry up, now, or we'll miss the plane. The pilot's an old friend of mine from Springfield, Massachusetts, and he always takes off on time."

Even with the burden of two suitcases, his easy

stride was quick and long, and Thea had to trot to keep up with him. Once again she was reminded of a cat in motion. Then a thought occurred to her.

"Wait! How do you know we're going to the same place?"

"The only thing in this direction is Ionian Airways. That's where I'm heading. And you?" For one instant he looked unsure of her destination, and Thea thought that she read disappointment in his face.

"Yes, that's where I'm heading, too," she said breathlessly.

"Melinas or Thribes?" asked the "god."

"What?" she asked distractedly. She had been staring at the lithe, muscular movements of the stranger's thighs as he walked several paces ahead of her.

"Which island are you going to visit, Melinas or Thribes? The six o'clock flight only stops in those two spots."

"Melinas," Thea said quickly. Evidently he had made this trip before. She wanted to ask him which island he was going to visit, but before she could question him, they arrived at the exit door. A wizened old man in a blue cap held it open for them, and they walked out of the cool building into the burning sun of an Athenian August. A small twin-engine plane was already running, and Thea's heart sank in dismay. The plane looked vintage World War II. If this was the only plane to Melinas, maybe she should have gone by boat.

The stranger saw her stricken expression and laughed. "Don't worry. It will get us there in one piece."

They walked along the steaming asphalt toward the plane. At the door, the "god," as Thea had mentally dubbed him, set down the bags and with a quick movement helped her up the shaky steps. At his touch she felt a flash of heat course through her body. And as she climbed the stairs, she was all too aware of his gaze lingering on her long, tanned legs. More than aware—she almost *felt* his caress on her skin. Gratefully, Thea saw that she was alone on the plane. She would need a moment to compose her burning face.

The stranger did not follow her on board. As she took one of the four window seats, she saw him stride over to a man in slacks and a polo shirt. They shook hands eagerly, and Thea guessed that this must be the old friend from Springfield. He looked competent, but she still gave a silent prayer that the plane would get them to Melinas.

Some minutes later, an old lady dressed entirely in black hobbled on board. Her gray hair was tied back in a bun, and the severity of her dress was relieved only by the large silver crucifix around her neck. To Thea's great amusement, she carried an enormous cheese in her arms like a baby. She smiled, revealing a few missing teeth.

"*Kali Mera.*" She nodded. Good day.

A thrill of delight soared through Thea. She was truly in Greece!

She glanced out the window at the stranger, who was still talking to the pilot. He had removed his jacket, and Thea could see more clearly now the taut muscles of his body as he moved his arms. For one wild moment she had the urge to remove his shirt, to see what his skin looked like underneath the civilized clothes he wore. Once again, the image of a powerful Greek god flashed through her mind.

As if sensing her eyes on him, he turned toward her window and gave a slight wave. For one second her heart plummeted. Perhaps he had changed his mind and wasn't coming on board. The thought upset her, but she was more irritated with herself. Why should she care?

Nevertheless, she breathed a small sigh of relief when she saw him head for the plane. There were six vacant seats on board. Which one would he choose? He didn't hesitate for a moment. As he sat down next to her, she felt the heat emanate from his body, and once again the subtle scent of the sea tantalized her nostrils.

After seating himself comfortably, he turned to her

with a smile, his white teeth bright against the dark tan of his face. His dark eyes were still filled with amusement as he put out his hand. Looking down, Thea noted the neatly trimmed nails and blunt fingertips.

"Nicholas Palmer," he said by way of introduction. "I'm also traveling to Melinas."

"And I'm Thea Hunt," she said, taking his hand. It was deliciously warm and hard.

Nicholas gave her a slow, easy smile. "Good. Now that the preliminaries are over, may I ask you out to dinner tonight?"

Chapter Two

Thea's large blue eyes grew even wider, but the impish smile on Nicholas' face banished any rudeness that the abrupt invitation may have implied. Nevertheless, the unexpected request caught her off balance, especially when she realized how much she wanted to accept. She thought quickly. Allie was going to leave a message at the hotel telling Thea when they would meet. Until she received word from her cousin, she wouldn't know what her plans were for the evening. To cover her confusion, Thea glanced down at her lap and noticed with a jolt that she still held onto Nicholas' hand. She released it immediately.

Thankfully, she had a reprieve before answering. The voice of the pilot came over the loudspeaker, telling them to fasten their seat belts. Landing time in Melinas would be in approximately forty-five minutes.

The little twin-engine immediately started down the runway, and Thea took the few moments of takeoff to try and gather her wits. Nicholas Palmer was certainly the most attractive man she had ever seen, and his impact on her senses was overwhelming. Her defenses lowered by jet lag, she wondered if she should even consider dinner with this man. She had an instinctive feeling that she would need all her wits about her when she was around him.

Her reprieve was extended as the little plane rose shakily into the air. For one terrifying moment Thea was positive that the plane wouldn't gain the necessary altitude and they would crash. She felt herself go pale with fright, and a gasp escaped her lips.

Then she felt Nicholas' warm hand over hers, reassuring and calm. "Don't worry. This is standard operating procedure for this plane. I'd be worried if it didn't shiver and shake."

Thea looked at him gratefully. "Thanks for the encouragement. I usually love to fly, but this plane makes me a little nervous."

"Perfectly understandable," he said with a chuckle. "I'm confident because I know the pilot so well. Mike Donell would never risk life or limb."

Thea was touched by his effort to put her at ease. She glanced down at the tanned, masculine hand which still covered hers protectively. She didn't want to let him go, yet she couldn't sit there holding hands with a stranger, even one as appealing as Nicholas Palmer.

But Nicholas released her hand himself as he leaned over her and pointed out the window. "Look there!" he commanded. His voice was low, and Thea could feel the caress of his warm breath on her neck. She shivered at the sensation.

Following the line of his hand, she saw the Acropolis bathed in sunlight. "My God, how beautiful," Thea whispered, the awe in her voice evident. "I had a quick view of it on the jet, but this is so much better. I feel as if I could reach out and touch it."

"It is magnificent," agreed Nicholas seriously. "Is this your first trip to Greece?"

"Yes," answered Thea, straining to get a last

glimpse of the Parthenon before the little plane swung out to sea. As it disappeared from view, she turned from the window with a sigh of genuine regret.

Nicholas smiled sympathetically. "Don't feel sad. You'll find that the entire country is wonderful. One minute you are in the twentieth century, the next moment back in the age of gods and goddesses." He leaned back in the seat and tried to stretch out his long legs in the cramped quarters of the little plane. Ruefully he gave up, crossed his legs, and continued. "The islands are incredibly beautiful. White stucco houses and vivid flowers surrounded by the blue sea. . . ."

There's a bit of the poet in him, thought Thea, listening carefully to his words. She liked that quality in a man. Strong, yet sensitive.

When he paused, she nodded. "I know. My grandmother told me so much about Greece when I was young that I really feel I've already seen it with my own eyes."

"Your grandmother was from Greece?" Nicholas' surprise showed as he glanced at her copper-colored hair.

"From Melinas," Thea said proudly. "I'm only half Greek. My father's family is Scots-Irish. But you seem pretty knowledgeable about the country. You must have been here before."

"Several times. Five to be exact," answered Nicholas succinctly.

"For business or pleasure?" asked Thea.

"Both. I came twice on vacation, and the last three times on business. I'm moving my business to Melinas." He paused. "And you? I assume this trip is for pleasure?"

Thea's heart skipped with excitement. "Actually, both. The pleasure will come from finally seeing the place my family used to own. But I have some business here, too."

Thea hadn't planned to tell him, but when he raised one dark eyebrow quizzically she found herself explaining. "My grandmother's family home is up for sale. It's just a small house, but it's a place I would love to own. My cousin wrote and told me about it."

Thea thought she saw Nicholas frown for a second, but the expression disappeared almost as quickly as it came. Deciding that it was her imagination, she dismissed it from her mind.

Her enthusiasm for her plans made her plunge eagerly into conversation, and she responded happily to Nicholas' interested questions. Before she knew it she was telling him about the cottage, her career, and the founding of The Magnificent Mermaid. Breathlessly, she stopped with a laugh.

"I'm sorry, Nicholas. I don't usually talk this much. You just got me going on my favorite subjects."

His dark eyes were filled with admiration. "Don't be silly. I love enthusiasm in a person. You're an ambitious woman with interesting goals."

"Well, it all certainly fills up my time," Thea responded, shaking her head. "Sometimes I wonder if I don't overdo it, but I guess I was born with a lot of energy."

Nicholas' eyes met hers, and once more she felt a warm flush sweep over her body. "It doesn't seem to have left you much time for a man." His voice was low, but Thea heard the question in it.

She answered honestly. "At one time it did, but he and I went our separate ways."

"Were you married?" His expression was very serious.

"Engaged." Thea paused, wondering how much to say, and he misunderstood her silence.

"Don't tell me if it's too upsetting for you." His voice was gentle.

Thea laughed a bit ruefully. "Not at all. It was probably the most amiable breakup in romantic history. Now that I look back on it, I think I may just have mistaken friendship for love."

She was surprised to see Nicholas' expression register a curious relief at her words. It must be my imagination again, Thea told herself. She hesitated, not sure of what to say. Then she took a deep breath and asked boldly. "And you?"

"Never married, no ties." He said it simply, directly. "There were women, but it was never the right place, or the right time."

Thea glanced out the window, reflecting on his words. It was hard to believe that such an attractive man could have escaped marriage after all these years, and she had seen enough from her travels to know how easily a wedding ring could be removed for a short trip. Yet she knew instinctively that Nicholas Palmer was telling the truth. There was a quality about him, a strength, which made it impossible to believe that he would compromise with life, or with the truth.

Thea's gaze rested on his face for a moment; then she met his dark eyes candidly. The emotion she saw there left her breathless. Besides admiration, his look clearly contained something else. Desire. She couldn't help but recognize it, and the knowledge excited her.

Without thinking, she blurted out the first question that came into her head. "Tell me about yourself, Nicholas."

"From A to Z?" he asked with a laugh.

She grinned, realizing that he had recognized her ploy.

Nicholas chuckled softly. "Born in Boston, parents of the proper variety, educated at Harvard. My major was business; my hobby is sailing. That's about it."

Thea regarded his lean, intelligent profile shrewdly. "I don't think so, but it's enough for the moment. What is your business?" she asked curiously.

Now it was Nicholas' turn to grow animated. "I turned my hobby into my business. I bought a small sailing sloop about ten years ago, and started taking tourists out on jaunts from Nantucket."

"I thought I recognized something of the Yankee in your voice," Thea cried, proud of her correct guess.

Nicholas gave an agreeable shrug. "Probably. Except for short trips, I've lived on Nantucket for the last ten years."

"And the business?"

He smiled. "I'm happy to say, quite successful. I now own a small fleet of ten sloops and schooners. People are eager to charter boats for their vacations. If they desire, I also provide crews."

"So why are you moving your business to Greece?" asked Thea.

Nicholas leaned forward in his seat, eager to explain. "The tourist season in Nantucket is short. For quite a while now I've been thinking of moving the business to a warmer climate. But Florida and the Caribbean are inundated with charter ship companies. A few years ago I visited Greece, and I knew immediately that I wanted to relocate here. Since then, I've been trying to find just the right location."

"And you found it on Melinas?" asked Thea, intrigued with his excitement when he spoke of his work. So this explained the dark tan, the sinewy body, and the free and easy movements consistent with work on the sea.

"I think so," he said cryptically. Then he flashed her a brilliant smile that made every nerve in her body quiver. "You never answered my question, by the way."

"What question?" Thea frowned, trying to recall.

"Dinner. Tonight." He touched her hand lightly. "Please."

Time to make a decision. She knew that she wanted to accept. Thea bit her lip, considering, and decided to hedge a little longer. "I'd love to, but I was just considering logistics versus jet lag."

"Logistics? Do you mean your hotel versus mine, and taxis, and time, etc? . . ." Nicholas laughed with real humor.

"Yes," said Thea, wondering why he was so amused.

"All those trappings of civilization don't exist on Melinas. There are only four hotels in town, and they are all in the same square. And if I can guess, you are staying at the Ionian Inn."

"Yes," Thea answered in surprise. "How did you know?"

"Simple. Just about all Americans stay at the Ionian. The hotel next door has a large clientele of Scandinavians and Germans, and the other two cater to Italians and native Greeks on vacation."

Thea gave him a direct look. "I guess you must be staying at the Ionian, then?" She felt her heart miss a beat.

"Yes." And again, for one fleeting moment, she saw desire in his eyes, and her own body grew warm in response. Now her heart was no longer just missing a few beats—it was palpitating erratically.

They spent the last ten minutes of the trip chatting more casually, the electricity coursing between them kept under control by the proximity of the Greek peasant lady who suddenly began to talk excitedly. They surmised that Melinas was her home, for she said the word several times, speaking quickly in Greek and broken English, gesturing with the enormous cheese for emphasis.

Finally, Thea asked her to speak only in Greek, and by recalling the language she had learned as a child she was able to make sense of the woman's effusive comments.

"She says she's glad to be home," translated Thea to Nicholas, as the woman kept up her excited chatter.

"She could kill us with her cheese," Nicholas said wryly, as the old lady tapped her seat with the strong smelling food.

Before Thea could comment, she realized that the plane was beginning its descent to Melinas. "Look, Nicholas, there it is!" she cried eagerly. Down below, a white pearl was set against a backdrop of turquoise blue. As the plane dropped lower and lower, the pearl grew and grew, slowly revealing hills and beaches, then villages and houses. Then, at last, the island's runway came into view.

"Welcome home, Thea," said Nicholas quietly. "I

think you will love it here." He gave her hand another squeeze, and she suddenly felt safe and warm. It really did feel as if she were coming home.

Turning toward him, she was surprised by the look in his eyes. Nicholas was studying her, deep in thought, and there was something in his expression she couldn't quite read.

Before she could question him the plane glided to a halt, and the three passengers quickly disembarked. Immediately the sea air tantalized Thea's nostrils, and she eagerly inhaled the heady scent of sun, salt, and something delightful which she couldn't identify.

As if he were reading her mind, Nicholas took her arm in his and spoke. "It's the scent of the lemon trees. It envelops the island."

"This is going to be a wonderful trip," said Thea gaily. She was finally in Melinas! After all these years, her dream had come true.

In fact, she was beginning to suspect that more than one dream had come true. Her eyes rested on Nicholas, who was picking up both his luggage and hers. A fine film of perspiration made his expensive shirt cling to his body, revealing the tautness of his muscles as he moved. Although he wore conservative clothes, he gave off an aura of unbridled freedom, a feeling of independence and self-sufficiency which Thea found very attractive. A strong, confident woman herself, she found qualities of strength very appealing in a man. And Nicholas seemed to have these qualities in good measure.

She had to admit that part of her elation at being on Melinas was heightened by the knowledge that Nicholas Palmer was also on the island.

At that moment she was distracted by a small commotion near the stucco building that served as a terminal. The old lady from the plane was being greeted by at least a dozen people, all talking rapidly and kissing the old woman with joy.

"She's probably been gone for a week," said Nicholas with amusement, following Thea's entranced gaze.

Thea's voice was filled with the warmth of happy

memories. "I think you're right. That's the way it used to be when I would visit my grandparents. Greeks are extremely demonstrative people."

"And extremely passionate." Nicholas' dark eyes again held a considering look, and Thea felt a flash of heat race through the center of her being. Why did she find this man so exciting?

Perhaps it was due to her suddenly overactive imagination, or fatigue from the trip. Certainly, if there were a wild, Mediterranean passion in her, she hadn't discovered it with Robert Graham. His halting kisses and hugs had been only vaguely pleasant for her.

Face it, Thea, she told herself, it was disappointing. And yet, perhaps, could there be more? . . . The thought had often crossed her mind.

The warm way Nicholas was regarding her made that question again pop into her head, but she quickly pushed it aside. Thea knew that she was curious, but she also knew her own values, and they didn't allow for one-night stands.

She flicked a long strand of copper hair from her face and resettled her sunglasses in place. A brown Jeep was barreling toward them, and for one second she feared that the driver, a young, dark-haired man, was not going to stop. But to her surprise he did, not five feet from them, with a squeal of brakes that would have done proud a New York cabby.

"The local taxi," said Nicholas dryly. "Andreo meets all the planes. They tell me he's never killed a passenger, although a few ducks and chickens on the road haven't been quite so lucky."

"*Ne, ne,*" said Andreo eagerly, using the Greek word for yes. He jumped out of the driver's seat and enthusiastically helped both her and Nicholas into the Jeep. In less than a moment they were careening down the airport road, and Thea knew immediately that she was in for the ride of her life.

"How far is it to town?" she shouted to Nicholas as the wind flew through her hair. The radio was pound-

ing out the exotic beat of Greek bouzoukia at maxi-
mum volume.

"About ten miles," he called back, laughing. "But
don't despair, the ride is beautiful. The road follows
the sea coast, and the whole trip is really worth the
fright!"

Thea gave a feeble smile, for Andreo had just
missed a chicken in the road by only a tail feather. But
soon she saw what Nicholas meant. The road suddenly turned to the right, and immediately before them
was the vast blue expanse of the Ionian Sea. For one
electrifying moment, Thea was sure that they would
sail over the cliff and into the turquoise water, but
the Jeep swerved on two wheels, tossing Thea into
Nicholas' lap, and then veered down the road to
the south.

Thea quickly straightened herself, but not before
she became acutely conscious of the intimate impact
of her breasts upon Nicholas' hard, muscular chest.
Although it had only been for an instant, Thea felt
clearly the warmth of his body, and she heard his
sudden, indrawn breath at the contact. One of his
powerful arms had quickly reached out to steady her,
and after she straightened he kept his arm securely
around her. She stiffened slightly, confused by her
feelings.

Nicholas gave her an affectionate squeeze, sensing
her embarrassment. "You'd better accept my help, or
you could sail right out of this Jeep! You're too thin to
be securely anchored."

"Spoken like a true sailor," said Thea dryly. For
several minutes she was tense, unbelievably aware of
his arm around her. Her heart beat faster, and she felt
giddy. Yet there was something about Nicholas that
made her feel warm and safe. When Andreo made
another hairpin turn, Nicholas held her more tightly
and his thigh pressed against hers. Thea decided that
her heart was now racing faster than the Jeep.

But after a few minutes she relaxed, entranced with
the scenery around her, and was soon lost in the

beauty of the island. To the left the road careened down a sharp embankment to the rocky coastline fifty feet below. The rocks were naturally a pale off-white, but the early evening sun cast a golden hue on both the rocks and the turquoise sea. Between the road and the water were occasional gnarled trees, beautiful in their stark severity.

Her hunch that these were olive trees proved correct as they neared a tiny village comprised of only six stucco houses and a church. The trees were now grouped in groves, and Thea could see men and women picking the olives from the branches. Everyone waved, and Andreo leaned on the horn until they cleared the village. Chickens flapped in the air, dogs barked, and Thea gasped with fright for one moment as a baby lamb barely escaped from the path of the careening Jeep.

Finally they arrived in the town of Melinas. A short time later, the Jeep turned into the village square, and Thea was amazed at the number of tavernas which lined it. People sat under gaily covered awnings, sipping wine, eating, and watching the world go by. The Jeep itself was obviously a nightly source of interest, sort of a Greek version of the evening news. Thea tried to ignore the interested looks cast their way, but once again she was aware of Nicholas' arm around her shoulder. It certainly looked as if they were arriving as a couple.

The Jeep pulled to a stop at the far side of the square, in front of the Ionian Inn. Nicholas helped Thea from the vehicle, and they walked into the cool interior of the white stucco hotel, followed by Andreo with the luggage. As Thea searched for a tip, Nicholas gave her a small wave.

"Don't worry. I have it," he said quickly. Thea was about to protest, but she saw the look on Andreo's face and knew that he was more than satisfied. Accept it as a nice gesture, she told herself sternly.

She walked to the desk, where the small, rotund clerk beamed at her.

"Madam, may I help you?" he asked in perfect

English, his Greek accent only adding to the precise pronunciation of the words.

"Yes, I have a reservation. My name is Thea Hunt."

The desk clerk's expressive black brows shot up in surprise, and he quickly looked past her to the newspaper rack where Nicholas had stationed himself, casually reading a London paper. It was obvious to Thea that the clerk thought that they were together, and his confusion was apparent. Thea's reservation card had been marked for only one occupant.

Although Thea knew exactly what he was thinking, she was too embarrassed even to think of explaining. "Is there a problem?" she asked curtly. "I thought everything was in order."

At her abrupt tone the clerk quickly realized his mistake, and to hide his error he became profusely polite. "No, no, Miss Hunt. None at all. Just one moment, while I get your key and ring for the bellboy."

"And would you check for any messages, please."

"I'm sorry, Miss Hunt. There aren't any," the clerk replied.

He moved with Mediterranean slowness, and Thea began to fidget, nervously aware of Nicholas now standing behind her. She wondered if he would repeat his invitation for dinner, but she suddenly felt shy about turning around. The desk clerk's mistaken assumption had thrown her off balance. But when all her arrangements were complete and she turned to follow the bellboy up the stairs, Nicholas reached out and took her by the arm, a gesture not lost on the clerk.

"How about dinner in an hour?" he persisted gently, with a smile. "See the courtyard straight ahead? They serve dinner out there."

Thea hesitated. Out of the corner of her eye she could see the desk clerk looking at them with speculation. Suddenly, everything seemed to be moving too fast. "Perhaps some other time. I really feel tired from the trip."

Nicholas clearly looked disappointed, but he didn't press her. "Definitely some other time," he said firmly.

With a quick smile at Nicholas, Thea turned to the waiting bellboy. As they headed for her room, she studied the hotel with interest. The stairwell led to an outside balcony encircling the four walls of the building. All guests entered their rooms via the balcony. Below it, in the side courtyard, was a large fountain surrounded by trees and flower beds. Also in the courtyard, as Nicholas had pointed out, there were tables set up for dinner.

Her room was delightful, and she surveyed it with pleasure. It contained no air conditioner, TV or telephone and was very clean and simple. A blue and gold Turkish rug protected part of the floor. A double bed with a blue spread, a solid oak dresser, and a straight chair completed the furniture. On the dresser was a white porcelain vase filled with wild flowers. White curtains swayed lightly in the breeze, and Thea saw a lemon tree outside the window, which faced the village square. Its delicious scent filled the room.

Before the bellboy left, she ordered a Greek pita sandwich to be sent to her room; then she took a quick peek in the bathroom, breathing a sigh of relief. Her years of traveling had taught her that other countries didn't value plumbing as did Americans, but this room was more than adequate. With a grateful sigh, Thea turned on the taps and adjusted the water. A warm bath was definitely in order.

As the water filled the giant tub, Thea unpacked with the efficiency of an experienced traveler. The night was warm, so she set aside a light blue halter dress to wear after her bath. Once everything was in place, she tied up her hair and sank gratefully into the warm tub.

Idly, she thought of the reason for her trip. She had better check again for messages after she ate dinner. Aletha would probably try to contact her soon. Then her mind wandered back to Nicholas. A very attractive man, she thought, and a slight tremor of pleasure rushed through her. She realized that she was looking forward to seeing him again.

After a few minutes, Thea got out of the tub and patted herself dry. Carefully she sprayed her favorite cologne behind her ears and between her soft, up-tilted breasts. She studied her face in the mirror for a moment, then applied a light dusting of blue shadow the color of her eyes, and just a touch of blush to her high cheekbones. She was tanned, and her lips already had a healthy pink color, so she decided to forgo any more makeup in favor of a natural, under-stated look.

She put on panties and a pair of white sandals, and then slipped into the blue dress. Glancing in the mirror, she saw that the soft material clung nicely to her body. She reached back and pulled off her scarf, letting her copper-colored hair fall to her shoulders.

Suddenly she laughed out loud. Why was she going to so much trouble with her appearance when she was dining alone in her room? Was it perhaps because she hoped to see Nicholas later? She shrugged, a little irritated with herself. She was thinking entirely too much about that man!

Outside her door was a tray with her sandwich and some coffee, and Thea ate quickly, eager to go downstairs and check for messages. Once outside on the balcony she paused and took in the scene. It was almost dark, and the courtyard was lit only by the candles on the tables. The soft light, combined with the warmth of the night and the sweet fragrance of the flowers, created a romantic air.

She went downstairs, and approached the desk. The clerk, filled with Mediterranean admiration for feminine beauty, beamed at her with appreciation.

"Are there any messages for me?" Thea asked, giving him a bright smile. She was delighted with his approval.

"*Ne*, Miss Hunt. Yes. This note was dropped off about ten minutes ago. I was going to send it to your room."

"Thank you." Thea opened the folded paper and

recognized the handwriting. She quickly scanned the
note from Aletha, her expression changing from
pleasure to a concerned frown.

Dear Thea,

Forgive me for not seeing you tonight, but my
son fell from his bike and needed a few stitches in
his leg. Nothing too serious but I won't see you
until ten tomorrow. Dimitri has found out that
there may be a complication to the purchase of
your grandmother's land. But do not fret. I will
explain all when I see you.
See you at ten tomorrow at the hotel.

Love,
Aletha

Complications? Thea's frown deepened. What did
that mean?

"Bad news?" Thea's thoughts were interrupted by
Nicholas' voice behind her. She turned quickly.

"I certainly hope not. But I'll find out tomorrow."
Her eyes rested appreciatively on Nicholas. He had
changed from his dark suit to a pair of blue slacks and
a short-sleeved yellow polo shirt. He looked immacu-
late but casual, a look Thea liked.

"You look very nice," he said, studying her with
pleasure. "No one would ever guess you had been
traveling for over twelve hours."

"Thank you," said Thea, glowing at his words. "I
bounce back fast."

"Good! I like that in a woman." He flashed her an
engaging smile. "Look, I just finished dinner in the
courtyard, and I'd love to have you join me for an
after-dinner drink."

This time she didn't hesitate. "I'd love one."

Nicholas took her arm and led her out to the
courtyard. A man who closely resembled the desk
clerk rushed up to meet them, and soon they were

seated at a table near the fountain. After conferring
with Thea, Nicholas ordered a bottle of retsina wine.

Thea glanced around the courtyard, noting that
most of the tables were empty. "I guess the dinner
crowd is gone," she commented.

"On the contrary, it's still too early for most people
to dine," replied Nicholas, pouring the wine. "In
Greece many people eat their big meal at noon. Then
they siesta. The shops close and everything slows
down until around five. Then at nine or ten, people
eat a light supper."

"You're very knowledgeable," said Thea, impressed. She took a sip of her wine, and grimaced
slightly. "Wow, I'd forgotten how strong retsina is.
My grandfather used to drink it."

"Would you prefer something else?" Nicholas
started to signal the waiter.

"No," answered Thea wryly. "In some perverse
way, I enjoy the stuff, even if it does remind me of
turpentine. I guess it brings back memories of my
grandparents."

Thea suddenly paused, looking around in wonder.
All those stories that she used to hear so long ago.
The wonderful plans she and Yaya had made. And
now she was here.

Nicholas read her mind. "So you've accomplished a
dream," he said, his dark eyes carefully studying her
face.

"Not quite yet." Her thoughts returned to the note,
and she frowned. "My cousin says there might be
complications to the sale. I hope it's nothing serious."

She looked up as she spoke, and once again she
caught a shadow passing quickly across Nicholas' face.
And as before, the look was gone so quickly that she
almost thought she had imagined it. And, after a few
moments, she forgot about it entirely.

Thea found Nicholas to be an amusing and intelligent conversationalist. He regaled her with stories
about his sailing days in Nantucket, and as he talked
she thought about how comfortable he seemed to be

here. Although he was definitely a New England Yankee, she decided that he would probably make the transition from Nantucket to Melinas without much difficulty when he moved his business.

"Happy?" asked Nicholas, pouring himself a little more wine.

"Yes, and totally relaxed. I think it's a combination of good company, potent drink, and a sudden rush of jet lag. I'm not going to question it. It's too delightful."

"Good. Some things aren't meant to be dissected. It ruins the magic." Nicholas had settled back in his chair and was watching her closely over the rim of his glass. "Diana," he said suddenly, as if he had found the answer for which he was searching.

"What?" Thea looked up at him in surprise, her blue eyes widening.

"Diana, the goddess of the moon and the hunt. You remind me of her."

"I'm flattered to be considered a goddess, Nicholas, but why did you choose Diana?" said Thea, coloring at his compliment. He looked so attractive to her as he sat across from her. The courtyard was now lit only by the moonlight and the candles on the tables. The combination made everything so romantic, so soft. Thea realized that she was staring at Nicholas.

"That statue in the fountain is supposed to be Diana." Nicholas spoke softly, pointing to the beautiful marble nude. Thea studied the sculpture with embarrassed interest, conscious suddenly of how closely the body of the nude did resemble her own slim form. She looked at Nicholas. His expression left no doubt that he was contemplating her own naked body. When she picked up her wineglass, her hand was shaking.

"Are you cold?" Nicholas' voice was filled with amusement.

Hardly, Thea thought ruefully to herself. Instead, she answered flippantly. "I have the shakes, I think. This wine certainly is potent."

Nicholas arched one dark eyebrow, not fooled by

her explanation. To distract him, Thea spoke quickly. "Please tell me more about the statue."

"They found it when they were putting a new plumbing system in the hotel," Nicholas told her. "It was buried about ten feet below ground and, amazingly, was totally unscathed. The proprietors of the hotel made a deal with the government—they could keep the statue as long as it was on display to the public."

"You certainly did your homework," said Thea.

"When something catches my interest, I want to discover everything about the subject." He looked at her directly, his dark eyes intense. An electric current pulsated hotly through her body, and suddenly the night seemed filled with anticipation.

Thea looked down, afraid that her emotions showed too clearly on her face. Careful, girl, she told herself. This is a man who would be difficult to control.

"Goddesses aren't supposed to be afraid of mere mortals," murmured Nicholas softly, a light, teasing quality to his voice.

"Afraid!" Thea's denial was adamant. "I'm not the least bit afraid of you. There's a tremendous difference between being cautious and being afraid."

"Well, then, why must you feel cautious?" Nicholas' dark eyes were probing hers, demanding an honest answer. He leaned toward her, his lithe body emanating an aura of controlled sexuality.

Thea met his eyes unflinchingly, and she answered honestly. "You're a very attractive man."

"And that makes me dangerous?" Nicholas countered.

"Yes, it does," she breathed softly. "On an island like this, with a man like you, it would be easy to forget to be careful."

"And don't you think that I might find *you* dangerous?" The current of tension in his voice was unmistakable.

Thea glanced at him in surprise, thinking that he must be joking, but he was absolutely serious. "I didn't think of that at all," she answered candidly.

Thea met his gaze, and suddenly the humor of the conversation made her burst into laughter. Nicholas gave her a startled look, then smiled at her.

"My God, here we sit, two very dangerous people, enjoying a marvelous bottle of wine." Nicholas tried to make his tone sound serious, but failed.

"I know," Thea said softly. "It just sounded to me like the script of one of those old late-night movies."

Nicholas nodded his head in agreement. "I really felt I should have a sword in hand to help force you off into the night if you refused my advances."

He said the word "advances" slowly, bringing to mind all sorts of deliciously wicked pleasures. Thea couldn't resist. "And are you advancing?" she teased, leaning toward him.

He didn't answer her with words. Instead, very gently he took her hand in his and with a slow, deliberate movement brought it up to his face, pressing his lips to the open palm of her hand. So potent was the exquisite touch of his tongue on her skin that Thea felt that he had kissed her far more intimately. A shudder passed through her body. Her hand trembled, and his own grip on her soft skin tightened, holding her helpless against his mouth.

"Nicholas." It was a whispered plea.

He looked at her, his dark eyes unreadable. "I've been advancing ever since I first saw you on the plane."

Thea smiled softly in memory. "It was strange. When I looked up and saw you, it was as if I had known you before. I couldn't explain it then, and I still can't."

Nicholas shook his head. "Funny, I felt the same way. It was an instantaneous attraction."

"Perhaps we knew each other in a previous life," Thea hazarded with a smile.

"Maybe." Nicholas paused, a wicked look on his face. "Or maybe it's just my natural appreciation for a great pair of legs."

Thea suddenly remembered how her skirt had been hiked up, and she flushed, not so much from modesty as from the memory of his warm glance on her thighs. Caution, she told herself again, smiling in spite of everything.

"What are you thinking about?" asked Nicholas, lifting her hand once again to his lips.

"Nothing." She paused, trying to catch her breath. "I think, Nicholas, that it's time to go. I have an early appointment tomorrow."

A smile played at the corners of his mouth, but he nodded in agreement. "Of course. It is after twelve."

She and Nicholas went silently upstairs, and as they walked the length of the balcony, the intoxicating scent of lemon enveloped them. The sharp, tantalizing perfume heightened Thea's senses; she felt as if every nerve in her body was waiting, anticipating something marvelous. When they reached her door, she turned to face Nicholas, whose profile was outlined against the midnight blue sky. She felt him move closer until their bodies were separated by only the width of a silk thread.

She had meant to say thank you, but the words were silenced by the sudden pressure of his lips on hers. With one deft movement he pulled her body close to his and held her fast, his mouth caressing hers, first gently, then with more and more pressure. With tantalizing slowness his mouth began to trace a pattern down her neck, making her quiver at the sensations he was creating. Unthinkingly, she flung her head back, aware, once again, of the wonderful sea scent of the man.

One sinewy arm went around her waist, imprisoning her against the hardness of his chest. Thea was aware of nothing but the marvelous sensation of his lips on hers and of a weakness in her knees. If his grip hadn't been so secure, she would have fallen. His grip on her waist and bare back tightened, and she felt his entire body press into hers. Dimly, somewhere in the recesses of her mind, she knew that she should stop him, but the other part of her, the sensuous part, kept pleading for the pleasure to go on. Instinctively, her arms went around his neck, pulling him closer, and she felt, rather than heard, the animal growl in his throat.

Her abandonment seemed to arouse him further, and she felt him tremble. One of his hands cupped her breast, softly massaging her through the soft material of her halter dress. Thea's body responded eagerly. His lips followed his hand, and Thea felt him pull back the restraining fabric. Then he moved to the cleft between her breasts, teasing and tormenting her. A soft moan escaped her lips.

Again he murmured an endearment, something between a word and a groan of pleasure. A panther, she thought, her half-opened eyes fixed on the luminescent moon as Nicholas' tongue flicked upward to the tender hollow of her throat. She felt him shudder as her fingers eagerly caressed the back of his neck, and he murmured in her ear. "Unlock the door, sweetheart."

His throaty voice, heavy with desire, both enflamed her and brought her crashing back to reality. What was she doing? She had only met Nicholas this afternoon. True, she had felt an instantaneous rapport with him, almost a physical shock of recognition. Still, she knew that she had to wait. It was impossible for her to make love casually.

She pushed him back, her body trembling. "Nicholas, wait. Please. This is getting out of hand."

"You want me, too." He said it simply.

"I know," Thea answered honestly. "And believe me, I'm not being a tease. But . . . everything between us is moving so fast. . . ." She paused, trying to choose her words carefully so there would be no misunderstanding. She couldn't deny that she wanted him to kiss her, to hold her in his arms and caress her.

Nicholas' fingers stroked her hair. Thea's cheeks were still flushed from his kisses, her lower lip trembling as she groped for the right words. He could see the dark shadows under her eyes, the only sign of her long, demanding day. He gently cupped her chin in his hand, his lips gently silencing her.

Then he released her, though he still kept his arm possessively around her waist. "I understand, believe me. It's been a very long, but absolutely perfect day. So let's get some sleep."

Thea arched one eyebrow, not sure if he meant alone or together.

He met her look with a growl. "Don't tempt me, lady," Nicholas laughed, giving her an affectionate hug. "I said I would wait."

"Then you may wait for quite a while," said Thea flippantly.

He laughed again and released her. "Good night, Thea. Sleep well."

Damn, she thought. Why is his voice like a caress? "Good night, Nicholas."

Later, lying in bed, Thea studied the moon through the open window. It hovered like a pale yellow sphere suspended in the dark velvet Mediterranean sky. Such a familiar object, yet it appeared so different in Melinas than it did in the States. Here it really seemed a part of her universe, its powers truly able to affect her life.

She had planned this trip since childhood, and so many of the things she saw today were exactly as Grandmother Helene had described them. But she had never anticipated meeting Nicholas Palmer. Again she puzzled over the feeling of recognition, the strong sensation that she had known him before. Perhaps there would be more to this trip than the culmination of a life-long dream.

She smiled in the dark and made herself comfortable against the crisp, clean pillows. Here she was, at last in Melinas, and she hadn't thought about her land deal in at least six hours. Easy girl, she cautioned herself. Basically, Thea was too practical to jeopardize something so important, and she knew that when tomorrow came she would have to get down to work on the land sale. Tomorrow.

But what about tonight? Well, it certainly had been

a pleasure. Her eyes again drifted to the window, back to the moon. Nicholas had called her Diana, the goddess of the moon and the hunt. He made her feel desirable. It was a wonderful feeling, and she wanted him as much as he wanted her. As she drifted off to sleep, she began to wonder who was doing the hunting, Diana the goddess, or Nicholas, the panther.

Chapter Three

Thea awoke before the travel alarm went off, brought to full alertness by the vibrant Greek sun splashing through her open window. A quick glance at the clock assured her that it was only eight-thirty. She had an hour and a half before she had to meet Aletha. Lazily she stretched against the soft white cotton sheets.

She had slept like a log. Her evening's activities must have left her even more relaxed than she'd thought. A little smile played around the corners of her lips. Perhaps relaxation wasn't the right word. Certainly the delicious excitement that shot through her body whenever she was with Nicholas couldn't be called relaxing. Nicholas. There was something about the man that both excited her senses and challenged her mind. It was a lethal combination.

Without intending to remember, she recalled in detail the evening they had shared, the conversation, the light flirtation masking the stimulating current of electricity somehow joining them together.

Dreamer, Thea told herself, half amused, half irritated. You should be concentrating on the land, not on Nicholas Palmer! Where is your business sense? She recalled the note from Aletha. A problem with the land sale, her cousin had written. What could it be? She debated several possibilities then dismissed the subject from her mind.

She would soon find out what it was, and she was sure that she would be able to solve the problem. It was inconceivable that anything could be seriously wrong. Filled with energy, Thea jumped out of bed and headed for the bathroom. Her mood was so bright that she didn't even mind the antiquated shower attachment over the tub. Instead of a full blast of hot water, she stood under a trickle of cool liquid. Local color, she told herself with a laugh.

Unbidden, the image of the marble Diana came to mind. Last night Nicholas had said that she reminded him of the statue in the garden. What would he think, now, if he saw her under the shower, her copper hair wet and in tangles, her body slippery with scented soap suds? Despite the cold water pouring over her, her skin heated with a warm flush. Just the thought of his eyes on her naked body had the power to arouse her.

Thea quickly tried to suppress the image. This is ridiculous, she told herself sternly. Nicholas was last night—she had business this morning! Determined to put thoughts of Nicholas aside, she rinsed herself off and stepped from the shower.

The rest of her toilet was completed quickly. When she was done, it was just a few minutes past nine. She had plenty of time for breakfast. As she walked out on the balcony, Thea glanced down into the courtyard. Her eyes raked over the guests sitting below. There was no sign of Nicholas, and she realized with surprise that she was disappointed. Somehow, she had been hoping to see him.

Keep your mind on business, she reminded herself.

Thea checked at the desk for messages, then went out to the sunny courtyard for breakfast. Her waiter was attentive and charming, and he brought her an American paper without asking. Thea smiled. The paper was two days old, but she didn't mind. The pace here was obviously a little slower than in the States.

She was on her second cup of coffee when she heard someone call her name. Looking up, she saw a pleasant-looking dark-haired young woman of medium height approaching. Her beaming smile told Thea immediately that the woman had to be Aletha. Thea jumped up, and in seconds they were in each other's arms.

They kissed and hugged, while two waiters stood nearby beaming in approval, their Mediterranean appreciation for all celebrations apparent in their broad smiles. After several minutes the two cousins released each other and stepped back, smiling.

"Thea, you are exactly as I imagined you would be. So American!" Aletha's voice was filled with emotion, making her Greek accent stronger than usual. Her dark eyes and plump cheeks were totally different from Thea's fair slenderness.

"And you, too, Aletha," cried Thea, her own blue eyes filled with tears. She and her cousin were the same age and had corresponded for years. Now they were meeting for the first time, and it was an emotional moment.

"Allie, call me Allie."

"All right, Allie," said Thea. "Do you want some coffee, some breakfast?"

"Coffee would be lovely. Thank you." Allie sat down, and a waiter quickly appeared, bringing another cup of the potent brew.

The two women regarded each other silently for a moment, then burst into giggles like two schoolgirls. "I still can't believe it," Thea laughed happily. "After all these years, to be here at last. Tell me, how is your family. Your son . . ."

"Fine, fine. Young Dimitri is just like his father, always getting into mischief." Allie's black eyes flashed merrily. And my daughter, Mavia, is a little *kukla.*" Allie hesitated, trying to remember the English word.

"Doll," said Thea helpfully.

"Yes, doll." Allie's accent was lilting and soft, very similar to the personality of the woman herself. Thea was delighted with her. They chatted for several minutes, until Allie's black eyes fixed on something behind her, and Thea turned curiously. Her heart jumped in her chest when she saw Nicholas in the doorway of the courtyard. He was dressed casually in blue jeans and a light blue shirt, and he looked marvelous. He was making his way over to them.

"Nicholas, I'd like you to meet my cousin, Allie," said Thea, quickly making introductions. She noticed the surprised admiration in Allie's eyes, and knew that her cousin was wondering what their relationship might be.

"I'm very pleased to meet you," said Nicholas.

"And I am so happy to meet you," Allie said haltingly, her black eyes sparkling.

"Would you like to join us for coffee?" Thea asked.

Nicholas looked disappointed. "Sorry. I'd love to, but I can't. I'm on my way to the docks." He indicated his casual clothes. "Today is a workday. But perhaps I'll see you later?"

Thea read the warm question in his eyes, and nodded, smiling. "Yes, fine."

Saying good-bye quickly, Nicholas left, and Thea looked at Allie a trifle sheepishly.

Allie's black eyes were now dancing with humor. "He is very good-looking, this American. So very handsome in the blue jeans. Only American men wear the blue jeans so well. Like a cowboy."

Thea laughed, both from embarrassment and from amusement at Allie's quaint English. "Yes, he is very good-looking. I met him on the plane. He's moving to Melinas."

"Aha," said Allie, raising her brows in sudden conjecture. Thea wondered how Greeks always managed to convey so much meaning in their simplest expressions. Allie obviously thought that there was more going on between her and Nicholas than met the eye. Then her cousin smiled. "Very nice, very nice.

Time for you to meet a very nice man, and a handsome one."

"Allie, not you, too!" cried Thea in mock anger, throwing up her hands in despair. "Really, he's just a friend."

"Perhaps 'friend' is a word I don't quite understand, but I think I see more than just 'friendship' in his eyes, and in yours, when you look at each other." Allie's dark brows again rose expressively. She was plainly enjoying this conversation.

Thea flushed. "I think you understand the word well enough."

"Aha," repeated Allie, nodding proudly at her correct assessment. For several moments she continued to tease her cousin; then she glanced at her watch. "I must pick up Mavia later, so why don't we start out now for a look at your grandmother's house and a meeting with the owner. My car is outside. We can talk on the way."

"Fine." Thea quickly paid the check and the two women left.

A trifle self-consciously Allie got into the driver's seat of the blue Volvo. "I just got my driver's license," she announced proudly.

"Great," Thea said, suppressing a nervous gulp. She hoped her smile looked genuine.

Allie pulled out into the village square, oblivious to pedestrians and traffic, and Thea was positive that her cousin must have attended the same driving school as Andreo, the cab driver. After a few moments Thea decided that the entire Greek population of Melinas must have enrolled in that school. The right of way went to the person blowing his horn the loudest, or shaking his fist and cursing with the most vigor. And everybody seemed to be enjoying themselves immensely.

To ease her nervousness, Thea spoke again. "What exactly is the problem complicating the land sale?"

Allie's face clouded over. "As you know, after your grandparents left for America, your great-uncle Peter lived in the family home. In 1972, when he was almost eighty, Peter sold the property to a man named John Prolisavis, who is now the present owner. John has decided to move back to Athens, and six months ago he approached my husband about buying the land. Of course, we were not interested, but we let you know immediately."

Thea held her breath as Allie executed a hairpin turn on the winding road leading to the west coast of the island. The Volvo made the turn safely, and both women breathed sighs of relief.

"I'm a very good driver, yes?" Allie said happily. Thankfully, before Thea had to answer, her cousin continued. "This is still a fairly poor island, and the price you offered John was better than anything any of the local people would give him. So, until last week, you really had the deal sewn up, as you Americans say."

"What happened last week?" Thea's voice held a note of fear.

Allie smiled ruefully. "Last week, another person made a better offer for the property. John came over and told us about the new offer, and asked if you could match it."

"What is the new price, Allie?"

"Eighty thousand drachmas."

"That's eight thousand dollars more than I offered," said Thea in dismay, as she quickly calculated the drachma-dollar exchange.

"Yes, that's about right." Allie's voice was disturbed. Then her face brightened slightly. "But you will talk to John this morning. He is a sentimental old man, and he would prefer to sell to you. Perhaps he will accept a little less."

"Who is the other buyer?"

Allie shrugged. "I don't know. But pay attention, now. Here is the beginning of the property. In a minute you will see both the house and the beach."

A short time later Allie turned off the seacoast road into a short drive, and Yaya's home lay before them. It was exactly as Thea had imagined it. At the end of the drive stood a white stucco house surrounded by a stone patio. Flower boxes filled with red and white geraniums made a beautiful contrast with the gray stone. The house stood at the top of small hill. The land sloped down to a rocky beach which bordered the perfect blue sea.

For an instant Thea couldn't move, so great was her emotional response to the place. Now that she had seen it, she knew that she wanted it more desperately than before. This was her land, her grandmother's birthplace. And she was going to fight for it. Her throat felt tight with unshed tears.

Allie's gentle words finally broke the silence. "I don't see John's car, but he said he might be late. He told me to take you right inside."

They parked the Volvo and walked up to the patio. A fat gray cat lay snoozing in the sun, and Thea rubbed him behind the ears. No wonder he was content. This place was like heaven. They walked around the patio to the front of the house, which faced the sea. Next to the door stood two more stone pots filled with flowers. A lemon tree gave a little shade to the front of the house, its soft scent enveloping them. It will be wonderful to wake up to this each morning, she thought, picturing herself on the stone patio with a cup of coffee.

Allie tried the door. It wasn't locked, so they entered. Once inside, Thea could no longer restrain her feelings. She smiled at Allie as tears finally escaped. This was the home she had learned to love as a child, and it was just as beautiful as she had imagined it—simple, but achingly lovely. The walls were white stucco, with a floor of dark gray slate. The kitchen and living room comprised one large room, which also served as the front entryway. A stone fireplace stood in one corner, and two windows looked out on the Ionian Sea. There was no glass in the windows, only blue shutters, which kept out the infrequent rain.

There were two small bedrooms, and Thea knew immediately that she would take the one facing the beach. And the bath was just as Allie had described, simple but functional.

"Let's walk down to the beach," said Thea impulsively after she had studied everything in the tiny house.

Allie eagerly agreed. Together they walked down the sloping hill to the little strip of sand. The water was an incredible shade of blue, a cross between turquoise and a shade of azure. She dipped her hand in it. It was clear and clean, and surprisingly warm. Thea licked the salt water from her skin. Her first taste of the Ionian Sea. Lovely.

She stood up and shaded her eyes, looking at the house on the hill. The blinding sunlight had bleached the stucco to the whitest of whites. Thea looked around her. Greece was a land of sunlight and color, especially white and blue. Blue for the sky and the sea. She loved it.

"I think I heard a car," said Allie softly, not wanting to intrude on Thea's thoughts.

"Terrific." Thea's voice was jubilant. She couldn't wait to iron out the problems that were holding up the land sale. Allie had trouble keeping up with her as they marched up the hill and entered the house.

Almost immediately after them a small, rotund man entered, greeting them and apologizing profusely for his lateness. "Excuse, excuse, hello, excuse me, Allie, madame, I late, I sorry."

Allie quickly made the necessary introductions.

"Pleased to meet," he said warmly, shaking Thea's hand. But Thea read concern in his dark eyes, and she felt his unease. Clearly, he was a nice man who was in the midst of a dilemma.

Nervously he offered them coffee, which they declined. Then he indicated that they should sit down at his wooden kitchen table. After a few moments of trial and error, they found that the easiest way to communicate was to have Allie translate from Greek to English, and then back for the sake of their host.

As they talked Thea's heart sank slowly in her chest. She had been dismayed at the original price of twenty thousand dollars, but she had been prepared to go to twenty-eight thousand to match the amount of the second offer. But as John slowly explained his predicament, she realized just how desperate her situation really was.

"The other party wants the land so badly that he will overbid any offer I get from others," Allie translated slowly. "This land is needed to complete a business deal. The other party has purchased the adjoining property to the left for almost one thousand feet along the shore. The American will pay any price to get my land.

Thea looked at John as Allie spoke, and very slowly a terrible thought began to formulate in her mind. The American will pay any price to complete the business deal. . . . What business deal? What American? She had a sinking feeling in the pit of her stomach.

"It is needed, my land, for a small business enterprise. Actually, not so small. The American will build a marina and charter boats to tourists. It will really help the people of Melinas, and I am a poor man. I could use the money. I would prefer to sell the land to you, of course." John looked at the ceiling, as if pleading for divine inspiration.

"And who is the American making the offer?" Thea took a deep breath, bracing herself for the answer.

John understood the question, and answered himself. "The American? His name is Nicholas Palmer."

Allie and Thea rode back to the hotel that afternoon in silence, Allie afraid to say anything and Thea bursting with impotent frustration. She could gladly strangle Nicholas. He must have known from the beginning that the land she wanted was the property he was trying to buy. She had said he was dangerous! Little did she know how dangerous! A vision of herself and Nicholas on the balcony kissing came abruptly to mind. Her cheeks became even redder at the memory, and she felt angry and humiliated.

"Thea," began Allie gently, "perhaps he didn't know. Sometimes these things happen. It will all work out."

"You bet it will," snapped Thea. "There's an old Yankee saying, 'He who laughs last, laughs best.' Well, I'm going to laugh last!"

Allie looked a little unsure of Thea's words. The rapid-fire English was too much for her. But she recognized turmoil when she saw it, and she realized that Thea was certainly as emotional as any full-blooded Greek. Poor Mr. Nicholas Palmer, Allie thought nervously. He was going to be in for a hard time.

Allie dropped her off at the entrance to the Ionian Inn, and Thea walked quickly up toward her room. She wanted to be alone to think, to calm down. But luck was against her. Nicholas stood near her door, pacing restlessly back and forth. Thea stopped dead; her first instinct was to turn and run. She didn't want to see him now. But before she could move, he turned and saw her.

"Thea," he cried, moving toward her quickly, his face tight with worry.

"How could you! You knew all along that you were trying to buy my grandmother's land," Thea hissed as he approached, her blue eyes almost black with anger at how he had deceived her. "I can't believe you would do such a thing."

Nicholas' expression was grim, but his voice was controlled as he followed her to the door of her room. "I didn't know, Thea. I suspected, but I was hoping that it was a different piece of land. I didn't find out until today, after I left you. There are quite a few lots up for sale, you know!"

"Then buy another one," said Thea quickly. "You don't need this particular lot!" Her heart pounding, she put the key in the lock of her door and pushed it open. Before she could stop him, Nicholas followed her inside the cool, darkened room, and shut the door.

"Yes, I do." Nicholas' voice was weary as he

continued the conversation. "I've already bought the land to the left of that lot."

"It isn't fair." Thea's voice shook. She was close to tears, but she wasn't going to let him get the best of her. It was bad enough that he was her rival for the property, but to also take advantage of what she'd begun to feel for him . . ."

Nicholas read her thoughts in the look on her face. "Thea, I swear to you I didn't know for sure. I prayed it wasn't true. The minute I saw you, I knew you were something special to me. I would have told you if I'd known."

"And now, I suppose, you think I will just forget my claim, and give in to you." Thea spat out the words.

"From what I've seen of you, I wouldn't think that for a minute," said Nicholas dryly. He reached out to touch her shoulder, but she flinched and pulled away.

Thea didn't try to keep the sarcasm out of her voice. "Then what do you suggest we do? Throw dice to see who gets the land?"

"Thea, let's just discuss this calmly." Nicholas' voice was stony, but Thea heard, and chose to ignore, the note of pleading underlying his tone."

"What can we discuss?" She clenched her hands in helpless frustration. "I travel thousands of miles to fulfill a lifelong dream to buy back my family land, and find instead that I've been outbid by a man I thought was my friend. And I believe you knew all along."

"That isn't true." His cold, clipped words revealed his tension. Before she could move he caught her arm in an iron grip. Angry as Thea was, she was still startled by the pain she saw in his eyes.

"I don't believe you," she said half-heartedly. To her horror, she felt tears start to well up in her eyes.

Nicholas saw them, and his expression turned from one of hurt to stark concern. "Thea . . ." He moved to pull her close, but she brushed his hand away.

"Please, leave me alone." A feeling of sadness was replacing her initial anger.

"No, I won't." His voice was brittle. "Not until you believe me. I would never set you up like that."

Something in his voice compelled her to look directly into his eyes. And what she saw written there was the truth. She knew it instinctively. He hadn't known. He hadn't just used her. But even as relief flooded through her, she was consumed with disappointment. They were still rivals fighting for the same land. That fact could not be swept away.

Wearily, Thea looked down at the floor. She needed time to think. "Please, Nicholas. Let go of my arm."

"Let's talk . . ." Again the pleading in his voice was real, but Thea was still too upset to care.

"There's nothing to discuss. Not now. Please, just leave me alone. I really need time to think."

Nicholas stared at her helplessly for a moment, then nodded coldly. Once more he looked to her like a Greek god, but this time an angry, frustrated one. All he needed to complete the image was a thunderbolt in his hand. With another curt nod, he turned abruptly and left the room.

As the door clicked shut, Thea sank wearily onto the bed, her temples aching from frustration and disappointment. Not only was she upset about the possible loss of the land, but she was amazed at how upset she was over Nicholas.

You hurt, admit it, she told herself. She had really fallen for Nicholas Palmer. The physical attraction had been immediate, but as soon as they had started talking the bond between them had become something more. Never in her life had she felt so inexplicably drawn to a man. She couldn't explain her immediate feeling that she belonged to him, belonged with him.

Now, that feeling no longer existed. No, that wasn't true. Unfortunately, it was as strong as ever. But she didn't want it to be so. They were rivals fighting for the same land. And neither one could win without hurting the other.

Weariness and frustration began to replace her

anger. Dispiritedly she flung off her shoes, and lay down on the bed. She tossed the problem over and over again in her mind, trying to find a solution, but there were no answers.

She recalled her last comments to John Prolisavis. She and Nicholas were caught in a trap. John had indicated that he would rather sell to Thea, but Nicholas' offer was so much greater, so much more tempting. John had asked for time to think. Ten days, and then he would give them both his answer.

Thea was not a napper. She rarely slept in the afternoon, even while on vacation. But now her frustration, and disappointment made her unbearably tired. She closed her eyes, just planning to rest, but in a few moments she fell into a troubled sleep.

Chapter Four

A light tapping sound woke her. Thea sat bolt upright, for one moment confused by her surroundings. The hotel room was shadowed, with only a faint light coming through the window. Somewhere in the distance she could hear music and laughter. She rubbed her eyes, trying to get her bearings, and the memory of her argument with Nicholas came flooding back, washing over her like a wave of cold water.

Again Thea heard the tapping, and with a start she realized that someone was at the door. She jumped up, hastily straightening her skirt and hair. Damn, what if it were Nicholas outside? Thea hated to be caught off balance. For a moment she debated whether to answer the knock, but decided she was being silly. She took a deep breath and opened the door.

Thea could barely see the little messenger boy behind the huge bouquet of roses and carnations. The little boy said hello in English, then held out a card with her name on it. Thoroughly puzzled, Thea took the beautiful flowers in her arms, pausing to inhale their compelling, aromatic scent. Lovely. Then she reached for the card.

The note was written on expensive blue stationery in strong, masculine handwriting.

Diana,

Even rivals need not be enemies. Cocktails at seven, if you dare.

Nicholas

Even as anger at his impertinence flared through her, she had to smile at his ruse. He knew that a challenge to her courage would entice her to go out, and she had to admit that his plan was working beautifully.

She hesitated, staring at the note. As the little messenger boy waited patiently, Thea debated the wisdom of answering Nicholas' challenge. Seeing him again would only complicate matters further. Perhaps she should decline.

Then Thea looked down at the flowers in her arms, and in spite of her good intentions a soft smile crossed her lips. She really wanted to go. In fact, it might be a good thing. Even though she wouldn't be able to outbid him for the land, keeping the lines of communication open between herself and her rival was a very good business practice. She considered her problem for one moment more, then asked the boy to wait.

While counting out a tip she toyed with the best way to answer Nicholas' invitation. Then inspiration hit her, and she reached into the dresser for some hotel stationery. She thought for a moment, then wrote down a few lines in her easy, flowing script.

Nicholas,

Of course rivals need not be enemies. I'll meet you in the lobby at seven.

Diana

She smiled, pleased with herself. By meeting him in the lobby she would be starting them off on a more equal footing than if he picked her up in her room.

She turned back to the boy, who was waiting with Mediterranean patience. "Mr. Palmer. Can you find him?"

"*Ne*. Yes, miss," the boy said happily, nodding his head for emphasis. "He is in his room."

"Good. Then please take him this note right away." Thea handed him the note and the drachmas. At his surprised and delighted look, she wondered if she had miscalculated the rate of exchange, but she smiled and waved the boy away, closing the door with a happy hum.

Her eyes rested on the flowers lying on the dresser. They were beautiful. It was a lovely thing for Nicholas to do, and again she saw the gentler side of him. She was suddenly, inexplicably delighted.

Thea glanced at the clock. It was close to six. She had plenty of time to get ready, but she wanted to create just the right impression. If Nicholas could be sophisticated and casual about this whole mess, then so could she.

Sophistication. Yes, that was definitely the feeling she wanted to convey. They were involved in a messy dispute over land they both wanted, but civilized people behaved in a certain way. She knew that she could handle it.

Carefully she went through her small wardrobe, considering and discarding dresses, until she came to a cream-colored sheath made of very soft jersey. It had a slit up the side, revealing a lot of thigh, and Thea decided at once that it was the perfect dress for an evening like tonight.

Then an ironic smile made its way to her lips. She knew how alluring the dress made her look and feel, and she had to question her motives for selecting it. Was it just to look sophisticated? Not really, she thought. She still wanted to impress Nicholas.

Admit it, she told herself. No matter what has happened, you still are attracted to the man. The problem isn't his fault any more than it's yours. And you still want him to find you beautiful and feminine.

Her exuberant mood momentarily wavered as she began to toy with the logistics of their problem, but with an impatient gesture she waved her thoughts aside. No. She wasn't going to get any more upset about this than she already was. In fact, she was going to enjoy herself. She would keep things cool and under control, but still have a good time. At least for tonight.

After dabbing a few drops of perfume behind each ear and between her breasts, she donned her panties and a pair of high-heeled navy blue sandals, finally slipping into the jersey. Then she studied herself in the mirror. The cream color of the dress accented the honey color of her tan, and was the perfect shade for her copper hair. She looked golden.

She also looked sophisticated and slinkily sexy. Thea was pleased. Last night an innocent, tonight a woman of the world. At least externally, she giggled to herself. She hoped that Nicholas would be caught off guard, and reconsider his rival. Sometimes a little psychological advantage didn't hurt.

She caught the reflection of the flowers in the mirror, and she turned toward the beautiful bouquet. On impulse she pulled out a red rose. It was just the right shade to catch and hold the brilliant copper highlights of her hair. With a smile she tucked it into her neckline. It was a perfect foil for her tanned, high breasts.

She was ready. She quickly picked up her purse and checked to make sure that she had her hotel key. Then she hesitated. She wanted to hurry downstairs to Nicholas, but suddenly she was nervous. Being with him had seemed so simple yesterday, but today the situation seemed infinitely more complex. Could she really pretend that their dispute didn't matter?

Thea stood in the middle of the room, filled with doubt. Then she sighed, tossing her copper hair back with resolution, and headed for the door. This was silly. Of course she could handle this situation.

Thea walked outside and listened with delight to the sounds of laughter and music coming from below. She peered over the balcony rail, but the courtyard was deserted. I wonder what's going on, she mused, forcing herself to think of the music, rather than the next few minutes. Her heart was beating rapidly as she headed for the lobby, but she gave herself a mental pep talk. *Simmer down. This is your business rival you're going to meet. You need a cool head.*

Thea walked into the lobby and immediately saw Nicholas. He was pacing back and forth with his back to her, but as soon as she entered the room he seemed to sense it. Turning quickly, he strode eagerly toward her, his eyes darkening in appreciation as he took in the sight of her.

"Very nice." The words were brief, but the huskiness of his voice conveyed a deeper meaning.

Thea smiled. Against her will, her heart raced at the sight of him. He was dressed casually in khaki slacks and a madras shirt open at the throat, and he looked marvelous.

She kept her voice light. "You look rather like a Greek god yourself."

"Thank you." His voice had become even huskier, and Thea saw a small muscle twitch in his cheek. His black eyes settled on the rose she wore, and Thea could see him considering her breasts, as if unable to draw his glance away. She suddenly felt naked, and though he made no effort to touch her, she felt the tension he was keeping in check. Memories of last night flooded her mind—Nicholas teasing and caressing her. She felt herself go crimson as a flash of heat surged through her body from both embarrassment and excitement.

Abruptly she tried to break the spell he was weaving around her again. "Thank you for the flowers. They were lovely."

His eyes widened in delight and he smiled. "Really? I'm glad you liked them." His sudden boyishness caught Thea off guard. It was so unexpected in such a sophisticated man.

This time her voice was less stilted and her smile more relaxed. "It was a lovely thing to do, Nicholas. But you didn't have to."

"I wanted to send them." His voice was firm, in control again. "You looked so upset when I left you. I couldn't stand to think of you being so unhappy for any length of time. I walked through Melinas, thinking about you."

Thea looked down, confused by his honesty. They were business rivals. He shouldn't care so much about her happiness. Before she could look up, she felt the touch of his hand under her chin, and he gently turned her face up to his.

Now his eyes were twinkling. "Come on. Let's enjoy ourselves tonight. Business can wait until tomorrow. Is it a deal?" His voice was warm, coaxing.

To say anything else but "deal" would have been rude. Thea smiled, her face showing her genuine pleasure. "You got a deal."

"Good." Nicholas' voice was firm, but relieved. "Let's join the celebration."

"Celebration,?" Thea was puzzled. That must explain the music and laughter she had heard from the balcony.

"Celebration," Nicholas repeated as they walked into the warm summer night. "I'll tell you all about it. As the saying goes—'There's a hot time in the old town to night.'"

He took her arm protectively, and Thea's skin tingled where he touched her bare arm. Why did this man affect her so? she wondered. It was as if a current of heat drew them closer and closer whenever they were together.

Suddenly she realized that Nicholas was speaking. "What?" she asked, looking up at him.

He looked down at her, a small smile on his lips. But his eyes were questioning. "I said, I thought we could have our drinks out in the square. Tonight is a special night in Melinas."

"So you keep saying," Thea said. "Are you going to let me in on the secret?"

"If you're good." Nicholas' expression was mischievous, and his hand tightened on her arm ever so slightly.

"You're not playing fair, Nicholas," Thea teased back, matching his light mood.

"All's fair in love and war."

"And in business," Thea replied, the words slipping out before she could stop them.

Nicholas looked at her with surprise, then shrugged. "If you say so."

Thea read the hurt in his eyes and cursed herself for her rudeness. This whole mess was not his fault! Impulsively she stopped and faced him. "I'm sorry, Nicholas. That was a low blow. I apologize."

Her words were sincere, and they reached him immediately. "Accepted and forgotten. Although I may make you pay. Later." His dark eyes were bright with laughter, and suddenly he reached down and gave her a kiss on the lips. "Come on. Don't look so upset. Tonight we're going to party."

The little outburst broke the tension, and they turned into the plaza with light hearts. Sure enough, the crowd milling about was even greater than usual. Nicholas drew her closer, protecting her from the laughing, jostling throng, and they made their way toward the center of activity. All the tavernas lining the square were filled with people. At the center of the plaza was a park with a fountain, benches, and a flower bed overflowing with colorful blooms. The park was small, but today several Greek bands were there playing folk music, and many of the milling people were dancing to the exciting beat of the bouzouki.

Several young Greek sailors strolled by them. One gave an appreciative whistle and said something in Greek.

"What did he say?" asked Nicholas, whose Greek was not quite good enough to catch the rapid exchange.

Thea's face colored slightly. "He said I had great legs."

"He has good taste," said Nicholas, but his voice held an undercurrent of jealousy and Thea was surprised to see him frown. It was as if he felt that she was his property, not to be looked at by any other man.

But before she could analyze his reaction he steered her to a table in a nearby taverna. A colorful awning waved in the night breeze, and the outdoor tables were lit with lanterns. The flickering light added to the festive mood. The sound of the bouzouki carried clearly to the patrons. They pulled their chairs close together so they could both face the crowds.

Thea happily tapped her foot to the demanding beat of the music. "I guess you must be right. This certainly seems to be a special night."

Before he could answer her, a waiter appeared and took their order for two glasses of wine. They watched the crowds for a moment before Thea turned to look at Nicholas. He had been watching her, his dark eyes studying the contours of her face. Once again his glance made her feel as if she had been caressed.

Once more she tried to break his spell. She took a sip of wine, and smiled. "Well, are you going to tell me?"

"What?" For once he seemed distracted, confused, and it made Thea feel better.

"What is going on here tonight?" There was gentle amusement in her voice.

"Oh, yes, the celebration. Hard to forget, right?" His voice was wry.

"Right. Just a little hard to miss. Unless you can overlook several hundred dancing, laughing people." Thea's tone was light.

But Nicholas was serious. "When I'm with you, I think I could overlook a thousand stampeding elephants."

Thea looked away, suddenly shy. "Nicholas, the celebration. Please!" She was firm.

"Okay, okay." He settled back, getting comfortable. "Tonight is the feast of St. Constantina of Melinas, a Greek Orthodox saint who was martyred during the time of the Crusades. When a Moslem fleet attacked the island, Constantina saved the lives of many of the children of the island by hiding them in a cave by the sea. The Moslems captured her, and when she refused to reveal the whereabouts of the children, they killed her."

"That certainly isn't very pleasant." Thea felt an immediate sympathy for this woman who had died so bravely hundreds of years before. She looked over the crowd thoughtfully. "And it certainly seems like an odd way to honor a saint. I know we Greeks are prone to celebrating, but this does seem a bit too much."

"It gets more interesting." Nicholas paused, taking a sip of his wine. He was relishing her curiosity.

"Come on, Nicholas." Thea's voice was slightly exasperated.

"It seems that the Moslems attacked on a day that had been sacred, in pagan times, to the goddess Diana. Even though Greece had become thoroughly Christian, the people of the island always celebrated the Day of Diana. So the date of the attack took on an even greater significance; this is not only a saint's day, but a pagan holiday. The day always falls on the first full moon in August."

Thea glanced up at the early evening sky. Although it was still light outdoors, the moon was starting to become visible. "What a lovely coincidence," she whispered, enchanted. A day for both a goddess and a saint.

An old man at the next table had overheard their conversation, and now he interrupted with an apology. "Excuse please, but I heard your story, and there is more to the legend. Diana and Constantina are also linked by that same spirit of self-sacrifice." He nodded enthusiastically, eager to tell his tale.

"Oh, yes," said Thea. "Please, go on."

The old man pulled his chair closer. "Legend has it that Diana, the goddess of the moon and the hunt, fell in love with a mortal, a handsome young prince, who wanted to be the king of Melinas. Diana wanted the island for herself, and she and the prince fought bitterly over the land. But when their love grew, Diana decided to marry the prince and share the island. This enraged Zeus, the king of all the gods and goddesses. He ordered Diana to leave Melinas forever, except for this one night of every year, when she could return, take on mortal shape, and visit her lover. If she refused, Zeus would take her lover's life and send him to the underworld."

Thea sat spellbound, listening to the tale. "Did she refuse?"

"No." The old man's eyes were sad. "She loved him too much to see him die. So she left the island forever, except for this one night each year. Legend says that she meets her lover in the cave by the sea. And in her hand she carries the rose the exact shade of the moon, a shade of gold so pale it can only be a gift from the goddess. She gives the rose to her lover, and when she leaves, the flower turns to gold in memory of her sacrifice for him."

"Beautiful," breathed Thea softly, entranced with the legend.

"If you go to her temple," continued the old man, "you'll see the golden rose worked into the mosaic of the floor. It is very lovely. And it is tradition on this island for young women to give their lovers a yellow rose as a token of their love. We grow a variety of roses on Melinas which is almost gold. It is beautiful, and it has a wonderful scent."

"Where is the temple of Diana?" asked Nicholas curiously.

"In the same cave where Saint Constantina hid the children. In fact, it was an archeologist sent by the Greek Orthodox Church who first discovered the little temple in the back of the cave. In ancient times the cave was a place of worship to the goddess. Today it is a very interesting spot for tourists. Anyone can tell you how to get there."

Thea began to shift nervously in her seat, suddenly thinking about how closely this tale paralleled her own situation. Not completely, because she was only attracted to Nicholas, not in love with him. Still . . . She glanced at Nicholas, who had also caught the similarity and was looking at her with amusement.

"How much did you pay him?" she asked dryly.

"Not a drachma," he laughed, throwing up his hands in a very Greek gesture of innocence.

His imitation was so clever that Thea burst into laughter, much to the amazement of the old man, who wasn't able to follow their rapid-fire English. Seeing his confusion, Thea reached out and patted his hand. "Thank you so much for telling us about the legend. We really enjoyed hearing it."

Before she could say more, one of the bands burst into a lively song, and she smiled at Nicholas with delight. He was looking at her with a half smile on his lips, his eyes warm with admiration, and in spite of herself she was thrilled by his obvious approval. Damn, she thought to herself, if only they didn't have the land dividing them. Suddenly she had a delicious desire to reach out and touch the dark, curling hair on his chest, made visible by the open neck of his shirt.

Her eyes lingered on his skin until she suddenly realized that she had been staring. She started guiltily.

"What were you thinking about?" he asked softly, his fingers brushing her wrist.

Thea flushed in irritation at her own stupidity. When would she learn to keep up her guard? "I was thinking about the land sale," she said quickly, trying to cover her confusion.

His dark eyes flickered with disappointment, and he sat back slightly. "Can't you forget the land for one moment?" His voice was harsh.

"It means too much to me," answered Thea defiantly.

"It means everything to me," Nicholas said coldly, "but I can still manage to think of something else."

"Well, good for you!" Thea's words were brittle. If

she had had the time to analyze her feelings, she would have known that her anger was half over the possible loss of the land and half over the frustration she felt in being so attracted to Nicholas, the cause of all her problems. "Perhaps you are more disciplined than I am."

"I doubt it." Nicholas' hand reached out and covered hers, and Thea shivered at the warmth of his fingers on her skin. "Thea, listen. Let's not fight over this property any more tonight."

"Do you have any idea how much I have wanted to own my grandmother's house?" Thea suddenly burst out, her voice quivering with emotion. "Ever since I was a little girl, I've dreamed of someday buying her old house. Now, to come so close, and possibly have it spoiled, is almost more than I can bear!"

"And do you know how long I've dreamed of moving my business to these islands? How I searched and searched until I found the right spot?" Nicholas demanded, squeezing her hand until she gave a little cry of pain. He didn't realize his own strength, and he was filled with frustration, trying to make her understand his predicament.

"You want the land for sentimental reasons, but I need it for my livelihood," he continued. "That piece of land changes my adjoining property from just a fair location to an excellent one for my business. The water off your grandmother's beach is very deep, and I will be able to anchor boats that I wouldn't be able to handle at the other spot."

Thea studied him as he stopped for breath. There was no doubt of his sincerity. He really needed the land. Her lips twisted into a slight smile. "I guess it's a question of sentimentality over practicality, isn't it?"

He looked at her closely, trying to find sarcasm in her words, but he found none. "I guess that's it."

"So what are we going to do?" Thea asked helplessly. "You want the land, I want the land. . . . How do we solve this dilemma?"

"I wish I knew," Nicholas said seriously. Then he

gave her hand another, more gentle squeeze. "But nothing can be solved tonight, and besides, I think it's pretty much out of our hands right now. John Prolisavis will be the one to decide who will get the land. And that decision won't be for several days. So why don't we call a truce for tonight, and just forget about our problems? Agreed?"

"Agreed," said Thea after a moment's thought.

"Instead, let's just talk about the good things between us."

Thea looked at him and smiled. "Like what?" she asked.

"Like the fact that I find you very beautiful, and I'm glad you are with me tonight." Nicholas' voice was low, and his eyes were darker than soft black velvet.

Thea looked down at their hands, unsure of what to say. "Nicholas, don't you think this will make it all the more difficult? . . ." She really didn't want him to stop looking at her that way, but this was dangerous territory.

"You agreed not to mention the problem between us." His voice was low, insistent, and Thea felt a slight throbbing in the pit of her stomach, a wonderful, unsettling feeling.

"I agreed," she admitted, "but you're taking unfair advantage of the situation."

"By telling you how lovely you are in that dress, and how I have a wild desire to take you in my arms and kiss you."

Thea could still hear the pulsing bouzouki music in the background and the laughter of the holiday crowds, but it seemed very far away. She was conscious only of Nicholas' eyes on her face as she searched for a response.

It was the waiter who saved her. The handsome young man freshened their drinks and asked to take their dinner order.

"Would you like dinner?" asked Nicholas calmly, as if nothing vital had just passed between them.

Thea was surprised to find that she was hungry,

then realized that she had not eaten lunch that day. "You know, I could eat something light."

The waiter smiled. "I think we have just the thing. It's our appetizer tray, but really, it is more like a small meal. Perhaps you would care to try it?"

"Sounds good to me," said Nicholas.

Thea glanced around the plaza, surprised to see that the moon was rising. In response, the sky was turning a darker shade of blue. Colorful lanterns, looking like miniature moons, were hung around the square, and now they threw off a warm, festive light.

She turned back to Nicholas, who was still holding on to her hand. "This really seems like a magical place, doesn't it? My grandmother told me stories about this feast day, but I had forgotten them."

"I don't know if this is a magical island, but tonight seems like a magical night," whispered Nicholas, toasting her with his wineglass.

Thea laughed in delight. "Why, Nicholas, I'm surprised. I would never have suspected that you'd say anything so romantic."

His face flushed in embarrassment. "Didn't think it was in this Yankee captain, did you?" he said a little sheepishly.

"Actually, I was thinking more of a pirate than a Yankee captain. Yankee captain sounds too respectable."

"And I don't look respectable?" he countered, cocking one dark eyebrow.

Thea laughed. "Yes, you do. But underneath the Boston facade there's something more. If you had lived two hundred years ago, you would have been more at home out on a whaler than in the polite drawing rooms of old Boston. You . . ." Thea hesitated, trying to find the right word.

"Yes?" Nicholas encouraged.

"You do remind me of a pirate," Thea blurted out, then flushed slightly at her own temerity.

But instead of being offended, Nicholas was at first startled, then overcome with amusement.

It was his full-hearted laughter that Thea could not resist. She started giggling, then together they laughed so hard that people around them began to smile in amusement, though they had no idea what was going on. But being Greeks, they naturally approved of high spirits and laughing lovers.

"Well, I hope you don't scare easily," Nicholas said, pretending to look stern.

"I don't scare at all," said Thea impishly.

Nicholas nodded in agreement. "I'll bet you don't! You probably were the meanest kid on the block."

"Probably," Thea agreed. "But I'll bet you weren't a little saint, either."

Nicholas nodded his head emphatically. "You could make a safe bet on that one. My poor parents had hoped for a future Supreme Court justice. Instead, they were glad to see that I managed to survive to adulthood."

Thea chuckled at the image of Nicholas as a child. "What made you turn to the sea?"

He grew serious. "I loved the ocean from the first day I saw it. We used to summer on the Cape, and I always swore that I would be a sailor. My parents prayed I would outgrow it, but their prayers weren't answered."

"That's just as well. I can't see you sitting on the bench, handing out legal judgments."

"Neither can I. I would have died of boredom." Nicholas grimaced. Then he looked at Thea. "What about you? How did you go into a business like the one you own?"

"Good luck. I was one of those people who just happened to make the right decision at the right time in my life." Thea paused thoughtfully, thinking about the early years of the business. "Carla and I were young enough to ignore the pitfalls, and our enthusiasm for the work carried us over the hard spots."

"I think you make a lot of good decisions. I don't believe that luck had too much to do with it." Nicholas was watching her closely.

Thea shrugged. "Not all my decisions have been so wise." She thought of Robert.

It was as if Nicholas could read her mind. "The fiancé?" He said the words as though they left a bitter taste in his mouth.

"He definitely was a mistake. But at least I corrected it before too much damage was done." Thea studied the rim of her wineglass.

"What did he do for a living?"

"He was a lawyer in New York."

"One of those sophisticated, worldly types." Nicholas' voice became brittle at the image he was conjuring. He could just imagine Thea in the arms of a debonair libertine, and the idea enraged him.

If Thea had been able to read his thoughts, she would have laughed at the image of Robert that he was creating in his mind. But unaware of the false picture he had, she continued speaking. "The experience taught me a lot." She was thinking about how important it was to really know a person's true desires before entering into a serious relationship.

Still looking at her glass, Thea didn't see Nicholas' expression become even darker. He had misunderstood her comment entirely, and his picture of Thea in another man's arms had become even more vivid.

Thea was still unaware of Nicholas' reaction. Instead, a half-smile of embarrassment touched her lips. What would Nicholas think if he knew that she was still a virgin after being engaged? It certainly wouldn't help her cool, sophisticated image.

Again Nicholas misread her entirely. The half-smile appeared to him to be the fond remembrance of another man's caresses.

At that moment Thea did look up, and she was amazed at his black expression. "Is something wrong?" she asked innocently.

Nicholas took a sip of his wine and tried to get control of himself. When he finally spoke, his voice was controlled. "No. I was just trying to imagine what he was like. What kind of a fool would let you go?"

Thea laughed. "A smart fool. I certainly wasn't what he wanted in a wife."

Nicholas' face plainly showed his puzzlement, but Thea decided to change the subject. But before she could think of a new topic, the waiter brought their food, and they settled down to enjoy the delicious fare. There were the inevitable and always excellent feta cheese, pickled peppers, and black olives. But the platter also contained other delicacies. There were grape leaves stuffed with lamb, rice, and spices, and tiny meatballs heavily seasoned with parsley.

Thea enjoyed every morsel, and grinned a little sheepishly when Nicholas caught her licking a crumb from her finger. "It's so good I can't bear to miss any of it."

"I know what you mean. I love Greek cooking. Would you like some dessert?"

"Heavens, no, but thanks. Coffee would be great, though."

"Turkish or American?" asked the ever-present waiter.

Thea hesitated, then decided. "Turkish."

The waiter returned with two little demitasse cups and a copper pot filled with a steaming brew. He poured a little into each cup, and the sweet scent of the coffee tantalized their nostrils. Turkish coffee, they were informed, had a sediment of grounds in the liquid, and so it was wise to let it sit for a few minutes to allow the grounds to settle.

"I know that what he says is true," Thea said after the waiter left the table. "My grandmother used to read the sediment at the bottom of the coffee cups, much like gypsies read tea leaves. She would drink her coffee, let the grounds dry for a while, then tell the fortunes she saw."

"Did she ever predict anything important?" Nicholas asked.

Thea looked at him seriously for a moment, then nodded. "Yes, she did. She said I would come to Melinas and live in her house."

A strange expression, almost of sadness, crossed

Nicholas' face. "Well, we'll soon find out how reliable the Turkish coffee school of fortune telling is."

"Yes." Thea didn't want to say more. Neither did Nicholas. The mood between them was again so pleasant, so warm. Tomorrow and its problems would come soon enough. By silent accord they decided to enjoy the night.

As if to signal their pact, Nicholas reached out and took Thea's hand in his. "It's a special night, isn't it, Thea?" His voice was low, searching, demanding that she be honest.

She looked up at him, again forgetting the hundreds of people surrounding them in the lantern lit square. The only person who held her attention was Nicholas. Once more she felt his magnetism, felt herself being drawn to him irresistibly.

"Thea?" He spoke again, and she knew that he needed reassurance that the problems between them had been set aside, at least for the night.

She smiled, bringing her wineglass to her lips, and she saw his glance linger at her mouth. "Yes, Nicholas, tonight is special."

He squeezed her hand. "I needed to hear you say that." Then, in an effort to break the intensity of the moment, he glanced around the plaza. "Do you want to take a stroll, and see what's happening?"

Thea agreed quickly, and Nicholas paid the check. With Nicholas' arm around her protectively, they eased into the celebration.

The crowd had grown larger and the mood more feverish as the moon rose. It now hung like a huge, golden sphere against a backdrop of dark blue velvet. Thea decided that the feast day of St. Constantina had more and more given way to the pagan holiday of Diana, ancient goddess of the moon. The bouzoukia were pulsating now with a faster, wilder beat, as if heralding the arrival of the goddess who was rushing to earth to meet her mortal lover.

The mood of the crowd began to affect both of them, and Nicholas' arm tightened around her waist as they walked through the throngs of laughing, dancing people. Although several different bands were playing, their combined sound blended into an intoxicating, sensuous beat which spurred the dancers to greater efforts.

They stopped in front of a small circle of dancers and watched as they formed a ring to perform a fast-paced round dance. The dancers waved to them to join the circle. Thea hesitated, unsure that she would remember a dance she had once known, but Nicholas pulled her forward with a laugh.

To her astonishment, he knew the steps and was surprisingly agile, even executing the complicated little twisting leap which ended each stanza of the song.

"Where did you learn how to do this?" she said, laughing as she missed a step and bumped into him.

"I was invited to a Greek wedding on my last trip here, and I learned how to do this dance and several others. I'm quite accomplished." His expression was pleasantly smug.

"You certainly are," Thea cried out over the music. She began to concentrate on the steps, and in a few moments she was moving along with the rest of them, stamping and clapping, and yelling at each turn. She felt the rose in her bodice suddenly come loose and drop to the ground, but she didn't try to retrieve it. The circle was moving too quickly, and in seconds the rose disappeared under the feet of the leaping dancers.

The song ended, and the band immediately moved into another one, this one with a slower, more sensuous beat which was more Turkish than Greek. The men moved back, letting the women alone glide to the erotic music, each woman creating her own small dance. Caught up in the moment, Thea began to sway her hips, delighting in the pulsating beat. She began to imitate the movements of the other women, though she presented a totally different picture than the Greek natives. Her copper-colored hair flew around her shoulders, catching the light of the lanterns, creating a golden aura around her head. The jersey material clung to her body, revealing her soft curves, and as she moved the slit in the dress exposed her long, tanned thigh. More than one man was watching her with interest, but when she turned at the end of the dance, the only person she saw was Nicholas.

He was watching her silently, his arms folded across his broad chest. His face was tense, and he was studying her every movement like a cat waiting to pounce. She looked into his eyes, and there was something ancient there, something primitive that couldn't be denied. It was the desire of a man for a beautiful woman. She knew he hadn't missed a curve or a turn of her dancing body.

"Very nice," he murmured thickly as she came toward him.

"Thank you." Thea's face flushed slightly at the memory of her abandoned dancing. "When in Rome . . ."

"Do as the Romans do," he finished for her. "But you do it better than any Roman, or should I say Greek, ever could." He slipped his arm possessively around her shoulder.

"I think you're prejudiced," Thea laughed, walking along with him. They began to move through the crowd toward a wine stand.

"I definitely am. But I think even Diana would give you the prize tonight." His arm was now tight around her waist, and Thea could feel his fingers through the soft jersey of her dress.

"Would you like some more wine? It's very warm."

"I probably shouldn't, but yes. I'm really thirsty."

Nicholas ordered two glasses from the wine vendor, and Thea gratefully sipped the cool, sweet liquid. There was no ice, but the wine was cool enough to be refreshing.

They strolled around, watching the celebrating people, happy and content in each other's company. It was a beautiful night.

Nicholas began to steer her across the square. Thea

was puzzled as to his destination, but he wouldn't tell her. Then the crowd broke, and Thea saw a flower stand straight ahead.

"You absolutely must have a flower," Nicholas said seriously.

Thea was touched. First the bouquet, now this. They stood in front of the gaily colored stall, and it was plain that Nicholas intended to choose the flower himself. It took him only a moment. Without hesitation he reached toward a vase of yellow roses, the exact color of the moon, and selected the most perfect bloom.

"Very good choice," the old lady who ran the stall said as she took the drachmas from Nicholas. "You picked the golden rose of Melinas, the flower of the goddess."

"I know," said Nicholas, turning toward Thea. "A perfect flower for a perfect woman. Diana's rose for my Diana." He handed her the long-stemmed bloom, and Thea inhaled the beautiful fragrance. She had never smelled a rose that had such a sweet, haunting scent.

She stood quietly, marveling at the soft, silky beauty of the petals, unsure of what to say. The rose's heady perfume combined with the gentle effects of the wine made her feel almost as if she and Nicholas were in another world.

"Do you like it?" His words were a caress.

Thea looked up at him, smiling. "Very much. You keep surprising me with the lovely things you do."

He didn't answer. Instead, he took her arm and started to walk slowly on the fringe of the crowd.

"It's getting even more crowded," said Thea, still feeling like she and Nicholas were in some strange way alone, even in the milling, laughing sea of people.

"Let's walk down to the harbor," he suggested, pulling her warm body closer to his. "We're only a short distance away."

Thea agreed, and they slowly began to follow the small, hilly street that led down to the harbor of Melinas. The moonlight was so bright that the stucco walls of the houses appeared to give off an aura of soft light. The moon itself hung over the ships in the harbor, wrapping everything in a magical glow. Thea paused halfway down the hill, staring at the incredibly beautiful scene.

"It's really easy to understand how the ancient people could see a beautiful goddess in such a moon," said Thea softly.

Nicholas didn't answer. Instead, he took her into his arms, his lips closing over hers with a demanding urgency that swept all thought from her mind. Somewhere in the distance she could hear the sound of the bouzouki, but it was the only external sound that penetrated her conscious mind. Everything else was centered on the taste of Nicholas' lips as his tongue touched hers. His arms held her in a powerful clasp, and suddenly she felt light-headed from the intensity of his kiss.

She moved her head slightly, dizzy with excitement, and he reluctantly released her, though his arm still surrounded her waist, the heat of his skin scorching her beneath the thin material of her gown.

"Come on," he whispered. "There's a spot I want to show you."

They walked down to the harbor, but turned away from the pier area, and moved instead toward an enormous rock standing nearby. Thea was amazed to find a little bench surrounded by a flower bed on the other side. It was a miniature park facing the water.

They sat down, and Nicholas smiled at her. "In the daytime, the sailors' wives come here to sit, waiting for their men to come home."

Thea was going to comment, but before she could answer him, he had pulled her close and was seeking her lips.

"I want you, Thea," he whispered against her hair. She could feel his warm breath against her face, and once again the faint, sexy scent of the sea came from his body. "I need you. I can't keep it inside any longer."

The sound of his voice, the feel of his touch, struck

a cord in Thea which she could not deny. She wondered if Diana's lover had been so arousing. Unable to stop herself, but not really understanding why, she put her arms around his neck, kissing him hungrily. Her response fired the desire that he was already feeling, and with a moan, he pulled her even tighter against his chest. She felt the fire between them, the passion which had been simmering for days, suddenly ignite into an inferno.

She wanted this man more than she had ever dreamed she could ever want a man. It wasn't just physical desire. It was something greater. She didn't understand it. It was a feeling, an intense emotion that made her recognize in Nicholas a desire that they join, become one. That emotion was now translated into passion, into this fire that was deliciously enveloping them both.

Was this the true moon madness people spoke about? she wondered as she opened her eyes and realized that they were bathed in the soft, wonderful light of the moon. Eagerly she arched her back as Nicholas' hand cupped her breast. Her nipples strained against the material that kept him from her skin, and she felt a low moan of desire well up in her throat.

Hearing her cry of passion, Nicholas pulled down the clinging material of the jersey. Thea felt his eagerness and heard his indrawn breath as he exposed one perfect white orb. She gave a little cry of ecstasy as his lips suddenly descended on the straining pink bud, encircling and teasing her with his tongue.

Thea was lost to all thought, and when he pulled away reluctantly she opened her eyes in startled disappointment. Unaware of how sensual she looked with one breast exposed, she sat up, searching Nicholas' face.

His hand reached out and stroked the back of her neck, and it was obvious that he was trying to control himself. Then he pulled her close, almost crushing her against his chest. "Thea, we can't make love here.

Not here. I don't want anything to disturb us when we make love. I want to lose myself in you."

Thea's head reeled, both from his caresses, and from his words. Everything was getting out of hand. Everything was moving too quickly. She shook her head, trying to clear it.

"What is it?" Nicholas sensed her confusion, and he drew back, puzzled.

"Nicholas, please." It was a cry from the heart. "I'm confused. I don't know what I'm feeling. I . . . I don't really know what came over me."

He studied her in the moonlight, the fever in his body just barely under control. God, how he wanted her. Why was she withdrawing from him? She almost looked . . . like she didn't understand what was happening between them. Almost like she had never made love before.

Could she possibly be a virgin? After all, she had been engaged, had almost married another man. Could she still be innocent? He wasn't sure.

As he sat silently next to her, his breath hot against her shoulder, Thea's own thoughts were in a turmoil. Could she tell him that she was a virgin? Tell him that she only wanted to make love to the man she would marry? Would he understand when her own voice betrayed the desire she felt within?

Finally he broke into her thoughts. "Is it because of the land deal? Is that what's bothering you?" His voice was quiet. There was no condemnation in it, only an aching need to know.

She started at the question. Thea hadn't thought of the land deal in hours. It would be simpler to let him believe that excuse, but she felt a compelling urge to tell him the truth. She hesitated, trying to frame her words, and as she sat there, her head resting against his shoulder, she could feel the strong, fast beat of his heart.

He mistook her silence for an unwillingness to speak, but he blamed himself. He had known from the beginning that she wasn't the type of woman who took sex lightly. It showed clearly in the way she held herself, the way she spoke. She was special. A passionate woman, he knew instinctively, but not one who gave free rein to those passions. He had rushed her. Not intentionally, but because he wanted her so desperately.

"Thea," he whispered, drawing her close. "Listen to me. I'm sorry. I got carried away." He gave a rueful laugh. "Believe me, with you it's really easy to lose control. But I'm sorry if I offended you, pushed you too quickly. It's just that . . . when I'm close to you like this, I forget everything but how much I want you."

"Nicholas, really, I'm not offended. I should be the one to apologize. I'm the one who lost control." Thea's voice was soft, her large blue eyes wide with concern.

Nicholas smiled down at her, his expression tender. "Well, I think it's a draw. We both lost control."

Thea laughed softly. "I don't know what came over me. It really must be the moon madness."

Something in her words made Nicholas look at her sharply, again puzzled at how innocent she seemed. After all, she must have felt a great deal for her fiancé. He assumed that they had made love.

"I think we had better get going. It's getting pretty late." Thea's words broke into his thoughts, and he dismissed the subject from his mind.

Nicholas rose reluctantly, pulling her to her feet. "I think you're right."

They walked slowly back to the hotel, taking the side streets bordering the harbor. The sound of the music and laughter reached them softly, only adding to the peace between them. Nicholas held Thea close as they walked, and they were silent, quietly sharing the beauty of the moonlight on the sparkling water. The little boats bobbed up and down, the gentle sound of the waves lapping against the wooden hulls adding to the music of the night.

It was far past midnight, and Thea thought of Diana. The goddess must be with her lover by now.

She lifted the golden rose to her face, and inhaled the scent, marveling once again at its haunting, other-worldly quality. Hearing her sigh, Nicholas pulled her even closer.

They reached the hotel, and Nicholas walked her up to her room. Just as she unlocked the door, he turned her to face him.

He hesitated for only a moment, then pulled her into his arms, pressing her body into his. But this time his kiss was gentle, and fire of passion kept tightly in check. As his lips pressed into hers, neither realized that they were silhouetted against the August moon, two lovers joined by the most ancient bond.

"It was a perfect night, Diana." His voice was low.

"Yes, Nicholas, it was." Thea looked up at him, smiling at his pet name for her.

"No longer rivals?" His voice was quiet, but there was an current of tension in it.

Thea hesitated. She wanted to answer honestly. She felt no anger toward Nicholas now. She finally spoke. "Not tonight, Nicholas. We weren't rivals tonight."

Nicholas looked down at her, his black eyes study-ing every line, every movement of her face. Then he nodded. "You're right. Not tonight."

In one swift movement, he kissed her lips, then he moved into the shadows. But as he disappeared into the darkness, Thea heard him call out, and she smiled.

"Good night, my Diana. Sweet dreams."

She entered her room and stood for one moment in the darkness, watching the moonlight. And she took a long, slow look at the rose in her hand. It had definitely been a magical night.

Chapter Five

Thea slept late the next morning. When she finally awoke, the strong Mediterranean sun was cascading through the sheer white curtains, highlighting everything in the room. She glanced languidly at the dresser, and found that it was already ten o'clock. With a sigh of gratification, she sank back against the pillows. After all, she really didn't have anything pressing to do today, and she *was* on vacation. It might be a good time just to relax and take in the sights—perhaps do a little shopping.

A dreamy smile played on her lips as she remembered the night before. What a special evening. Slowly she recalled every single detail, bringing back the magic with her imagination. Her blue eyes drifted to the bouquet of flowers on the dresser. In the center stood Diana's rose, still perfect in its golden simplicity. Thea inhaled the fragrant scent of flowers which pervaded the room and sighed; the flowers brought back the night even more clearly.

Thea closed her eyes as she tried to understand her wild, abandoned response to Nicholas, and his own desire for her. She had never experienced the feelings of passion he provoked in her, the unbelievable desire to become closer, to reach for something she didn't quite understand.

It wasn't that she was ignorant about making love. She had read all the right articles. But articles were all so clinical. They left you totally unprepared for the actual experience. It was like studying about an earthquake, and then actually experiencing one. All the reading in the world couldn't prepare you for the feeling of being lost in something greater than yourself.

With Robert there had been nothing comparable. His kisses had aroused her to affection, nothing more. But calm, even-tempered Robert was totally unlike Nicholas. Nicholas, who seemed to burn with a white-hot flame when he held her in his arms. Something about his savage response kindled a fire in her which could not be denied.

The feeling he created in her was like traveling in stormy seas. She knew where she should be going, but the current of her emotions seemed bent on carrying her someplace else, to an exotic land where she could get lost forever.

The ancient Greeks had believed in the Sirens, those magical women who lured sailors to their doom by singing haunting songs. Was passion like that . . . a Siren drawing you closer and closer, until you lost control and plunged right ahead, heedless of the dangers?

Against her will, Thea's thoughts drifted to the land deal, and she remembered her conversation with Nicholas as they were parting for the night. No, they hadn't been rivals yesterday. But now it was morning. Irritably, she brushed the thought away, unwilling to deal with it just yet. She was still basking in the golden glow of the night's celebration.

By now Thea was thoroughly awake. In a sudden burst of energy, she got out of bed and headed for the bathroom. She would take a quick shower, then go have breakfast. After she dried herself off, she looked through her wardrobe and selected a white cotton blouse embroidered in the peasant style, and a mid-calf cotton skirt of dark blue. With a pair of low-heeled sandals, it would be a perfect outfit for sightseeing.

Thea dressed quickly, spurred on by her sudden hunger. Breakfast sounded delicious. By a quarter to eleven she was downstairs in the deserted courtyard. It seemed like everyone else was sleeping late today. She had heard the celebration continue until dawn, so most people would be awfully tired.

It was a glorious day. Thea felt as if she were surrounded by sunlight and flowers, and it was hard for her to recall the magical moon. Everything was very beautiful, but very real, and Thea knew that the time for fantasy had ended. She could no longer push the problem of the land sale aside.

Thea thoughtfully sipped her coffee as she waited for her breakfast to be served. Actually, she didn't have any options at the moment, she realized. The land sale was really out of her hands.

A rather sleepy-eyed waiter brought her breakfast, and Thea decided that he must have had a little too much partying last night. She bit into a crusty roll without really noticing it. Her thoughts had turned to Nicholas.

The sun was shining, and the magic night was over. Thea knew that he would want to see her again, and everything in her responded in the same way. Now that she had met Nicholas, she found it hard to imagine never seeing him again. But she had to ask herself honestly if it was wise. They were fighting over the same piece of property, and it was land they both desperately wanted. One of them was going to lose, and it was going to hurt terribly. Wouldn't the pain be much greater if they became even more involved?

She stared into her cup, looking at the sediment from the coffee, and she remembered their conversation last night. They had talked about fortune telling. If only she could look into the cup and see the right decision. But life was never that simple. It was up to her alone to make the right move. And in the analytical light of day, it seemed like things could only get worse.

I guess that tells me something, she told herself with a rueful smile. A waiter standing nearby, who had been one of the onlookers when she had danced last night, wondered why the pretty lady now looked so sad.

Thea could have told him. She had decided to avoid Nicholas from now on. It would just be too difficult to continue the way they were going. The potential for hurt was too great. Her decision depressed her, but she knew that she was right. They should see each other as little as possible.

Well, what could she do today to stay out of his way? Thea thought for a moment and decided that her original idea of sightseeing in the market area would be a good way to keep busy. Before she had left New York, she and Carla had made their decision to import Greek crafts for the shop. Today would be a good day to make a study of what was available. And she also wanted to buy gifts to bring home.

Once her mind was made up, Thea acted quickly. Finishing her coffee, she beckoned to the waiter, who gave her careful instructions on how to reach the market area, which was within easy walking distance of the hotel.

She was filled with determination to occupy her time fully and not think of Nicholas, and at first she succeeded. The day was perfect. The sky was a beautiful, clear shade of blue found in few places in the world. There wasn't even the remotest hint of smog or pollution, and the wind from the sea helped alleviate the heat of the intense Mediterranean sun.

As she walked through the town she studied the architecture with interest. Most of the buildings were made of white stucco, but their sameness was altered by intense dashes of color. Lemon and orange trees lined the streets, and a few automobiles passed her, with almost every driver honking a greeting or calling out a hello. She had heard much from Yaya about the friendliness of the people, and was soon greeting everyone she saw with a smile.

Thea consulted her map and saw that she had to take a right hand turn to reach the marketplace, which was located near the harbor. For one moment she thought of Nicholas and wondered if he would be down by the boats. But as soon as the image of his smiling black eyes formed in her mind, she ruthlessly pushed it aside. She wasn't supposed to be thinking about Nicholas!

The street leading downhill to the harbor was mainly residential, and Thea slowed her pace even more to better study the architecture there. Almost every house had a walled garden with a gate, and Thea couldn't resist peeking inside several of the gardens. She could see flowers, and little fountains, and, once in a while she would hear people chattering away in Greek. The familiar sounds were an echo from the past, and Thea thought of her grandmother. A lump rose in her throat at the memory of her dear Yaya, but she quickly suppressed her sadness. Yaya, more than anyone, would want her to enjoy this day.

When Thea reached the bottom of the hill, she paused for a moment, taking in the lovely view. Ahead of her was the Ionian Sea. Today the water was almost turquoise, and the sunlight made everything seem bright and clean. Seagulls swooped out of the sky, picking up bits of food thrown by people on boats, and their piercing cries mingled with the shouts of the men working on the docks.

As Thea walked toward the marketplace, she studied the ships in the harbor. Many were small fishing craft, belonging to the local fishermen, and Thea could see dark, thin men working at winding rope, spreading out nets, and repairing sails.

Her quick eye also noticed that the harbor held many pleasure boats. Yachts from all over the Mediterranean were anchored in these waters, their white hulls a perfect foil for the blue sea. The billowing white sails of sailboats blew in the breeze, and Thea could see people lounging on their decks, taking advantage of the sun to work on their tans.

Nicholas was right. Melinas was definitely becoming a port of call for tourists. A boat charter company like the one he was planning would probably do very well here. Tourists who didn't own their own boats would be eager to rent one for their vacation.

Again she was thinking of Nicholas! Angrily, Thea brushed his image from her mind and tried to concentrate on the scene up ahead. Luckily, it provided a perfect diversion. The marketplace, unlike the plaza, was teeming with people. The shops were lined up facing the water. Some were actual stores, but the majority were stands with awnings, where vendors peddled their wares.

The noise was remarkable. Everyone was talking at once: the vendors, the local people doing their shopping, and the tourists with their cameras. Thea was delighted with the exotic commotion, and decided to explore everything carefully. She approached the first group of shops and stalls, and found that they were filled with fresh fish and meats. She didn't linger too long in this section. Farther along, oranges, grapes, lemons, and pomegranates overflowed in carts covered with red awnings. Beyond them were the olive stands, and then the cheese section. Thea wrinkled her nose at the pungent odors. Still farther down were the wine dealers, and she firmly declined the offers to sample some of their wares. All she needed was to get tipsy.

Finally she arrived at the area filled with the type of merchandise she might buy for her store. Taking a notebook from her purse, Thea began to carefully analyze the products. The first store carried sheepskin rugs, and Thea examined the quality and texture, plus the price. The rugs were handmade, and the workmanship was excellent. The price she was quoted was a little high, but that was set for tourists. She would be making an entirely different offer to the craftsman.

After a few questions in halting Greek, Thea

discovered that the old lady running the stand was the mother of the man who made the rugs. She eagerly gave Thea her son's name and address, and Thea jotted everything down in her notebook. She would get in touch with the man, and perhaps make a deal to import rugs into the States.

So her afternoon continued. Melinas had a large marketplace, and the hours passed quickly, as she checked goods and made decisions about merchandise. Around four o'clock Thea realized that she had finally seen just about everything, and was pleased with the success of her day. She had the names of four possible suppliers for the store, and she had also bought presents for the people back home. And she even bought a present for herself. After debating a few minutes, she had gone back to the first store and bought a sheepskin rug. It would be perfect in front of her fireplace.

Laden with her packages, Thea headed back up the hill leading to the plaza. It seemed much steeper than she remembered from the night before. The sheepskin rug was hot against her skin, and the bulky packages didn't help. By the time she reached the plaza, she was tired, hot, and thirsty. She shifted her packages carefully and looked at her watch. It was almost four-thirty.

The plaza was now filling up with people, and Thea looked at the tables and chairs with longing. It certainly would be good to sit down. On impulse she headed for the first taverna on the square. It was set back slightly, so she felt less conspicuous, yet she was still able to watch everything happening in the area.

After ordering a glass of wine, Thea sat back and slowly began to unwind. As she watched the crowds of people strolling along, the couples with arms linked as they crossed the square, she thought about how leisurely life was on Melinas. The standard of living wasn't high compared to that in America, but people seemed to enjoy the simple things in life: the sun, the water, a quiet stroll in the plaza, or just sitting in a taverna watching the world go by.

As she thought about how nice it would be to live on Melinas, her thoughts inevitably turned to Nicholas. Suddenly she missed him. When she had been busy it had been easier to keep him from her mind, but now, sitting alone, she could no longer hold back her memories. Less than twenty-four hours ago they had sat in this plaza, enjoying themselves immensely. Now she was sitting here by herself.

A feeling of loneliness overcame her, and she debated leaving. But it was almost dinnertime; she realized that she was hungry, and the thought of eating alone at the hotel seemed too depressing. And she might run into Nicholas. Although that was a tempting incentive to return, she remembered her vow to avoid him, and she knew that he would be looking for her. Better to eat at the taverna.

Slowly, savoring every bite, Thea began to eat the salad she'd ordered, trying not to notice that she was the only person sitting alone. Ordinarily this didn't bother her, but tonight she felt different. In this crowd of warm, friendly people, she felt her own isolation.

Finally she was done with her meal, and the waiter brought her a cup of steaming coffee. She was carefully stirring it when a voice broke into her concentration, and she jumped, spilling a few drops of cream on the red tablecloth.

"Mind if I join you?" Nicholas was standing in front of the table, looking down at her. He was dressed casually in jeans and a red cotton shirt. The jeans were a perfect fit, hugging the lean muscles of his long legs. The cut of his shirt emphasized the broadness of his chest and the trimness of his waist.

Thea flushed, both from pleasure and from embarrassment. Had he guessed that she had been avoiding him today?

"Of course not. I just finished dinner." Thea couldn't quite hide from herself the pleasure she felt at his arrival.

"I gathered that." There was a slight edge to Nicholas' voice.

Thea looked up at him in surprise, and he caught

her expression and smiled ruefully. "I was tied up with the cement contractor at my property all day, but I left several messages for you at the desk because I wanted to take you to dinner. But when I returned to the hotel the bell clerk said you had gone out and not returned. I waited around for a while, then decided to come looking for you."

In spite of herself, a small smile hovered around Thea's lips. She quickly tried to suppress the pleasure she felt in discovering that Nicholas had missed her. It wasn't playing fair, trying to avoid him, then being happy when he found her. Games like that were for children.

Nicholas sat down, stretching his long legs comfortably. He looked totally relaxed, but Thea felt him studying her carefully.

She took a sip of her coffee. "I went out at about eleven. To the marketplace. I wanted to check on some possible purchases for the store." She pointed to the rug and other gifts. "I also got some things for myself."

"Was it a successful day?" Nicholas sounded genuinely interested, and Thea told him about the dealers that she was going to contact for shipments to the States. Nicholas was an excellent businessman, and soon they were discussing the value versus the cost of making the orders, and possible trade restrictions that she might run into with the importation authorities. Before she knew it, they were talking intently and she was jotting notes down in her book.

It was almost nine o'clock before Thea glanced at her watch again. And then she remembered her good intentions about avoiding Nicholas. Well, this hadn't been a romantic evening. They had discussed business all night. But it *had* been very pleasant. Too pleasant. It was time to get going.

Nicholas looked a little surprised when she said that she was tired, but he made no objection to her desire to head back to the hotel.

"Please, you don't have to walk me back. The plaza

is crowded with people." Thea didn't want him to cut short his evening just because she was leaving.

"Don't be silly." Nicholas' voice was firm, and he took her packages from her as they stood. "I wouldn't dream of letting you walk back alone."

"I travel all over the world by myself," laughed Thea.

He gave her a serious look. "I know. But this time it's different. Now you're with me."

Thea didn't answer. His statement created too many questions, and she wasn't ready for the answers. Besides, it was nice walking beside him through the plaza.

"Besides, I don't want to take any chances." Nicholas' voice broke into Thea's thoughts.

"On what?" Thea asked curiously, tilting her head up to look at him.

"On not getting to make a date with you for tomorrow. I thought we could go out on my boat and do a little sailing." His eyes were twinkling with merriment. "I promise not to be a bad pirate and throw you overboard."

Thea looked ahead, desire fighting with good sense. "I don't think so, Nicholas," she murmured softly.

He leaned closer, trying to see her face. Then he stopped dead in his tracks, forcing her to a halt. "Then my hunch was right. You were avoiding me today?"

She saw the hurt in his eyes, and she felt awful. "I'm not avoiding you because I don't want to see you, Nicholas," she blurted out. "I'm just trying to make things easier for both of us."

"How is not seeing me making anything easier?" His voice was blunt.

"Because . . ." Thea groped, trying to find the right words. "We do have this problem between us. . . ."

"The land."

"Yes."

"But I thought we could still see each other." A

small muscle in his cheek twitched, revealing his tension. "In fact, I know we can still see each other. We shouldn't allow the land sale to affect us."

"But it will! Can't you see that?" Thea looked up at him, pleading for understanding.

Suddenly, the rug he was holding got too close to his face, and the delicate hairs made him sneeze. The response was too much for both of them, and they laughed, breaking the tension.

"Nicholas . . ." Thea's voice was determined, but she couldn't hide her laughter.

"Don't 'Nicholas' me," he said laughing, but he was equally determined. "Say you'll go sailing with me tomorrow. Otherwise, we're going to sit in the middle of the plaza while I sneeze until the sun comes up."

Thea bit her lip, trying to gather her wits. Nicholas looked so engaging, so handsome as he smiled down at her, that she gave in to her own wishes. "Okay," she muttered, pretending to be annoyed. "You win."

"Good!" he laughed, swooping down to give her a kiss. But the rug was too much for her, too, and she began to sneeze. Laughing together, they walked back to the hotel.

Chapter Six

Sleep didn't come easily to Thea when she returned to the hotel. She went to bed early, hoping that a good book would relax her and help her to sleep. Instead, her thoughts kept straying back to Nicholas. She really shouldn't have accepted his invitation to go sailing, but it had been too difficult to refuse. Especially since she really wanted to go.

When she finally gave up on the novel and turned the light off at eleven, sleep still eluded her. It was close to one before she finally drifted off, and she woke several times during the night, tossing and turning. She had set her alarm for nine, and was just waking on her own when the buzzer went off.

Thea showered and dressed quickly, putting on a pale blue bikini underneath a pair of white shorts and a navy blue T-shirt. After a moment's thought, she decided that sneakers would be better than sandals for boating. She had just pulled her hair back with a clip when Nicholas knocked on her door.

He looked marvelous. Like her he was wearing white shorts, but his T-shirt was red. His long muscular legs were tanned a deep brown, as were his arms. He could have been cast in a suntan commercial. He looked every inch the sailor.

"Good morning, ma'am. Ready for a day of sailing?" He was ultrapolite, mimicking his own official captain's voice.

"Aye, aye, sir." Thea saluted smartly.

"Good. I've got a thermos in the car, so we can have coffee on the boat."

"Terrific."

They went down to the red Volvo that Nicholas had rented for his stay on Melinas, and were soon down at the pier. It was Sunday, and the docks were deserted. In the distance Thea could hear the lovely sound of chimes as the churches on the island called to the faithful. Nicholas parked the car, and they carried the thermos and picnic basket to the edge of the dock. A little red dinghy was bobbing up and down in the water.

Thea looked blankly at the dinghy, not understanding. "Nicholas, I thought we were going sailing. This is a rowboat!"

Nicholas burst into laughter. "Have you ever sailed before?" he demanded, the twinkle in his eyes taking the edge from his voice. He stood with his hands on his hips, his legs spread apart, and Thea was again reminded of a pirate.

"No." She said the words defiantly, wondering what was so funny.

He pointed to a sleek schooner anchored about a hundred yards from the dock. "That, my little landlubber, is our boat. We take the dinghy out to the schooner. It has to anchor out in the harbor because the dock area is too small to accommodate pleasure boats."

Thea looked around, suddenly noticing that there were at least twenty other boats in the harbor area. She had seen them yesterday, but hadn't really questioned why they were all anchored so far out. Feeling a little sheepish, she smiled at Nicholas. "Do I walk the plank for my ignorance?"

"No. You just have to do all the rowing."

Nonetheless, once they were in the dinghy Nicholas took the oars and began rowing, the muscles of his arms rippling as he guided the rowboat out to the schooner.

"Is this your boat?" Thea asked once when they were aboard.

"No. Belongs to a friend. My boats are still all in Cape Cod. I'm going to sell them, and buy new ones."

"Why?"

"They aren't big enough to make a trans-Atlantic crossing. Not safely."

"Sounds like you have your work cut out for you," Thea mused, watching him put up the sails. He had ordered her to sit down and enjoy a cup of coffee as he got the boat ready, and it was obvious to Thea that he certainly knew what he was doing. In minutes he had put up the sails, stowed away their picnic lunch, secured the ropes, and lifted anchor. And then they were on their way, the offshore breeze catching the sail like an invisible hand, pushing them out into the Ionian Sea.

It was a beautiful morning. The sky was a cloudless blue, and the bright sun warmed them. The breeze was just right, strong enough to give them good sailing, but mild enough to let them relax. Gently they glided across the blue satin water. Nicholas handled the boat easily, tacking back and forth to catch the breeze, and as he worked he explained to Thea the intricacies of sailing.

Fascinated, Thea listened intently to everything he said. Finally, she asked if she could try her own hand at maneuvering the sails, and Nicholas agreed immediately.

She had one close call and the boat almost capsized, but Nicholas quickly rectified the situation, and they were soon back on course. Thea loved it after her initial nervousness was over, and she eagerly helped Nicholas, learning more and more.

"You're my best pupil," Nicholas said after she executed a particularly difficult move.

"I think you're a little prejudiced," Thea laughed, her face lighting up with pleasure.

"No, really. You have a real talent for sailing. I've spent hours with people trying to teach them the rudiments of handling the sails, and they've never got the hang of it."

Thea felt immensely pleased. Even if he was flattering her a little, she loved it. And she did think that she was beginning to understand the basics.

"You know, I've always had this dream of sailing around the world," she confided. "I've read about people doing it, and I thought it would be wonderful to try." She felt a bit foolish telling this to Nicholas, since she had never even sailed before, but he looked at her seriously.

"I've always wanted to try it, too," he said. "I've sailed across the Atlantic on a racing yacht, but that's as far as I've gotten."

"Did you have fun?" Thea's blue eyes were bright with interest.

"Yes, but it was hard work. I crewed for a man who was bringing his boat from England to Newport for the America's Cup Race. This was while I was in college."

Thea listened to him as he spoke about the trip, until he suddenly shaded his eyes, and looked at the horizon.

"What is it?" she asked worriedly.

"Over there, to starboard," Nicholas cried, pointing with his hand.

Thea had no idea that starboard meant to the right, but her eyes followed Nicholas' hand and she saw gray fins bobbing up and down in the water.

"Oh, my God, sharks!" she cried, fear constricting her chest.

Nicholas burst into delighted laughter. "Before you go around the world by boat you'd better be able to tell sharks from a school of porpoises. Sit down and I'll take the helm. We'll follow them."

Relieved and excited, Thea went back to her original seat and waited eagerly as Nicholas turned the schooner. They soon caught up with the school, and Thea watched spellbound as the porpoises leaped up from the water, arced, and then splashed back into the sea.

"They look like they're playing," she laughed as she observed their antics.

"They are." Nicholas was excited, too, but his greatest pleasure was in seeing the look of delight on Thea's face. "There's a lot of food in the galley. Get some crackers, and we'll see if they'll eat them."

Thea rushed to the hamper and found a box of saltines. There were at least eight playing porpoises, and she tossed some crackers into their midst as Nicholas moved the boat closer. To her amazement, two of the porpoises leaped into the air, trying to catch the food. One succeeded.

"Oh, Nicholas, I can't believe how friendly they are!"

"They're naturally friendly, and very intelligent. These porpoises are even friendlier than most. They're probably used to tourists feeding them. Try some more crackers."

Sure enough, the porpoises had quickly figured out that they were going to be fed, and when Thea threw out the second batch three of them managed to catch the crackers in their mouths.

Thea thought for a moment, then began aiming carefully and was soon throwing crackers to each individual porpoise. To her delight, each was adept at catching his particular portion.

"I can't believe it. They're beautiful." Thea turned toward Nicholas, who was watching her rather than the sea animals. "They look like they're smiling."

"It's the natural shape of their mouths. But it does look like a smile."

They played with the dancing school of porpoises for almost half an hour before the animals suddenly tired of the game and dove off, farther out to sea.

"They seem so free." Thea was straining to keep them in sight. Then she looked at Nicholas, who had turned to adjust a sail. The porpoises were part of the sea, creatures both wild and free. And so was Nicholas. He definitely belonged here, out on the water, sailing with the wind. It showed in all his movements, a perfect harmony with the currents of nature.

Nicholas caught her gazing at him, and he smiled, his teeth white against his dark tan. "A penny for your thoughts."

"Oh, no. At least a dollar," Thea teased him.

"It's a deal."

Thea smiled. It was hard to put her thoughts into words. "I guess I was just realizing how at home you are out here."

He looked at her seriously. "This is my life. My work. I wouldn't give it up for the world."

"I can see that." Thea was thoughtful, then suddenly sad. The conflict between them could seriously impair his plans if she turned out to be the one to win.

Intuitively understanding her thoughts, Nicholas changed the subject. "Why don't we drop anchor and go for a swim?"

Thea gazed into the inviting blue water. "Is it safe? Are there any sharks?"

"Not a one. I promise you. These waters are relatively shark-free. That's why tourists love to come here."

"Great." Thea began to pull off her T-shirt, but as she wriggled free of it she caught Nicholas' gaze on her body, and she suddenly felt shy. Although her bikini was only a modified cut, something about his riveting look made her feel naked. Trying to act nonchalant, she kicked off her sneakers. But when the time came to remove her shorts, she hesitated, toying with the buckle of her belt.

"Don't be shy with me, Thea." Nicholas' voice was low. "I won't hurt you." He felt a painful thrust of desire surge through him.

"I never thought you would," Thea responded, trying to make her voice sound light.

"You have a beautiful body. I can't help . . . admiring you." Somehow, he made the word "admire" sound like "desire."

Thea resolutely pulled off her shorts and stood before him, forcing herself to meet his gaze. He had removed his own shorts, and he wore a red racing suit. His chest was covered with a light matting of dark, curling hair, which moved gently over his stomach. He was beautiful.

"We can climb back up with this ladder," he said, securing it to the side of the boat with hooks. He had purposely turned away from her. Looking at Thea and not touching her was becoming extremely difficult. And he was painfully aware that his suit did little to hide his physical state. "But it might be easier to dive in. It's about twenty feet deep here."

Thea was used to diving, and she executed a perfect dive into the warm, inviting water. As she started to come up through the sea foam she heard Nicholas dive in, and she splashed around, waiting for him to surface.

"Like it?" he called to her after a moment.

"Love it!" She tried out several strokes, feeling delightfully buoyant in the salt water, then struck out at a good clip in a crawl stroke. She felt Nicholas move beside her, matching his pace to hers, and she suddenly thought of porpoises, who swam in pairs. That was what they were like, she decided whimsically. A pair of porpoises.

"Nicholas, this is wonderful," she sighed, stopping to tread water.

He didn't answer. Instead, he circled around behind her and took her in his arms. "Relax for a moment, and let me tread water for both of us. You sound a little winded."

"Are you sure you can keep us both afloat?" she asked, trying to quell her reaction to his warm arms around her waist.

"Positive."

And he was right. His long powerful legs easily kept them afloat, and against her will Thea sank back against his hard chest. She was feeling a little tired, she told herself. Slowly, ever so slowly, he started moving back toward the boat, and as he moved he began kissing her neck, pushing the wet tendrils of her hair out of the way. Thea felt a delicious thrill move up and down her spine, and instinctively she began to arch her back.

Nicholas moaned in response, and his arm around her waist pressed into her flesh, pulling her closer. "God, Thea, you make me want . . ." He stopped, trying to control himself.

Thea didn't ask what he wanted. His voice told her everything. But she didn't want to move away. The warmth of Nicholas' body, the warmth of the water, the sun on her face, all combined to lull her into a soft, gentle world of sensuous feeling. She didn't want any of it to stop.

It was Nicholas who, with a sudden growl of frustration, moved away, dunking her under the water.

"Nicholas," she sputtered, coming up for air. "Why did you do such a thing?" Thea was laughing and coughing at the same time.

"I thought we should both cool off." Frustration and laughter mingled in his own voice. They paddled around for a while, playfully splashing at each other, then Thea headed for the boat.

"Aren't you coming on board?" Thea cried as she climbed up the ladder.

Watching her wet, almost naked body moving up the ladder, Nicholas felt a desire even hotter than before sear through him. When she called out again, he shook his head. "I'm going to swim around the boat a couple of times. I think I better work off my frustration."

"Frustration?" Thea looked after him.

"Are you daft, woman?" Nicholas roared, then broke into a maniacal crawl.

Thea watched him for a moment. His meaning finally sank in, and, in spite of herself, she couldn't deny the feeling of satisfaction which enveloped her.

They sailed for another hour, slowly coming closer to shore to better see the sights on land. There were several magnificent villas on this side of the island, and Thea and Nicholas waved to the occupants of a small yacht that was heading for the private dock of one mansion. Farther along the shoreline, olive groves sloped down to the water. Nestled among the olive trees were the small stucco cottages of the farmers who tended the groves.

"Look, Nicholas! What's that over there?" Set back a few feet from the water was the entrance to what appeared to be a large cave. A Greek flag stood on the beach before it. It was the blue and white standard which had first caught Thea's attention.

Nicholas thought for a moment. "I think it might be the archeological site of the old temple of Diana. Someone told me that it was in this area. And the Greek government is doing an official excavation, so that would explain the flag. Hand me those binoculars."

Thea quickly located them, and Nicholas studied the cave. "Yes," he said after a moment. "It *is* the entrance to the temple. We could go ashore, but the sign says the site is closed today."

Thea's disappointment showed clearly in her face, but she shrugged philosophically. "Well, we can visit it some other time."

"Right. Besides, I'm hungry. Why don't we find a spot to drop anchor? We can row the dinghy ashore and picnic on land."

"Terrific." She suddenly realized that she was starving.

They sailed around for another half hour before they came to the perfect spot, an isolated cove with a sandy beach. It was hemmed in by a thick grove of olive trees, making it very private.

They anchored the boat and took the dinghy ashore, taking care with the hamper filled with food and a large beach blanket.

"Now, what delights do you have inside that hamper?" Thea asked when they were settled on the blanket.

"All sorts of surprises. I had the hotel kitchen make

up their picnic lunch 'par excellence.' Those were the chef's words, not mine." Nicholas opened the hamper. "Actually, I'm as curious as you are."

They weren't disappointed. There were tiny Greek meat balls, broiled chicken in lemon and butter, pastry filled with chopped beef, and little cheese cakes. Underneath it all was a plate covered with a red napkin. Thea removed it and found an assortment of Greek pastries. And nestled in the corner of the hamper was a bottle of red wine, and two glasses.

"Definitely *par excellence,*" said Thea, taking a bite of pastry. The beef had been seasoned with Greek cheese and parsley, and it was delicious.

"Some wine?"

"I'd love some," Thea answered, wiping a crumb from her hand. "Greek food is delicious, but spicy."

They were both starving, and they devoured everything in the hamper, chatting as they ate. Before they knew it, half the bottle of wine was gone, too.

"I think I'm in heaven," said Nicholas as he stretched out on the blanket, "or very close to it."

"I know. I feel the same way. Peaceful, drowsy." Thea closed the lid of the hamper and set it aside. Joining Nicholas on the blanket, she stretched out, happy to lie down and let the sun warm her body. The breeze from the sea cooled them just enough to make the temperature perfect.

They lay there for a while, content in their shared silence, watching the gulls swoop down to catch fish. The quiet was disturbed only by the gentle lapping of the waves and the occasional call of a sea bird. Thea felt her eyelids grow heavy, and she and Nicholas fell asleep.

It was a teasing tickle moving up and down her back which slowly brought her back to consciousness. Damn, what is it? she wondered protestingly, her body still reveling in the warmth of the sun. She tried to brush the offending tickle away, but it only started up again as soon as she began to drift off.

Thea sat up with a start and glared at Nicholas, who

had been gently trailing a long blade of sea grass up and down her spine.

"I couldn't help it. You were just too tempting." He laughed, ignoring her protests. "The devil made me do it."

"With you, Nicholas, I suspect the devil often gets the upper hand," Thea muttered.

"Yes, he does," said Nicholas seriously, waving the sea grass back and forth. His black eyes were watching her alertly. "He's always making me do things, but I rarely regret acting on my impulses."

"Rarely." Thea was still groggy, and she missed the growing gleam in his eyes.

"Very rarely."

He moved as quickly as a cat, and the next minute she was in his powerful arms, his hard, warm chest pressing into her soft, yielding breasts. His lips silenced the surprised little cry that rose from her throat, and she felt her own lips part in response to his eager, demanding mouth. Thea felt Nicholas' fingers caressing the hollow of her back, and slowly she felt herself sinking into a wonderful abyss.

Then reality returned with a start, and she tried to push him away. "Nicholas, please . . ." she cried.

"Why? You want me to kiss you, to hold you close." His voice was warm against her ear, though he loosened his hold on her slightly.

"Yes, I do," Thea replied honestly, still feeling the delicious sensations his hand had provoked against her sensitive skin. "But . . ."

"But what?" Now his tongue was exploring the silken spot behind her left earlobe, and he was wondering how anything could be so soft.

She pushed herself farther away. She had to stop the delightful feelings he was arousing in her. "This is only going to make matters worse between us. We have to face the truth. We can't get too close."

"Thea, if you're referring to the land, you're being ridiculous. The simple fact is that we're *already* close, and nothing can change that. I wish you would stop thinking about it, and relax." Nicholas' voice was firm, but Thea could hear his frustration at their situation, a feeling she understood completely.

"I'm not always thinking about it," Thea protested hotly. But she considered Nicholas' words. *We're already close.* Was that true? Of course it was. Without giving it a lot of thought, she knew that they were bonded in a way. In a special way.

Nicholas watched her expression alter, saw the troubled look on her face, and he gently cupped her chin in his hand. "Thea . . . you can't deny that there's something special between us. I've never cared about any other woman like this." His voice was velvet, warm and intimate.

Thea looked up at him, her blue eyes caressing the strong contours of his face, and with sudden, deep insight, she realized that she loved Nicholas. Really loved him. The realization was intoxicating. But with the self-knowledge came pain. Nicholas hadn't mentioned love. He cared about her. Caring and loving weren't the same thing.

He saw a sudden light cross her face like a shooting star, only to be followed by a look of tender sadness. His hand reached out and wiped a grain of sand from her cheek, and he pressed her gently against the blanket. Drawing her into his arms, his tongue teased the corner of her lips.

Thea wanted to blurt out the truth—I love you— but she forced herself to keep silent. She wouldn't burden him with her love. Her wide blue eyes opened as she looked up at Nicholas' tanned, handsome face, and she met his eyes trustingly. "Yes, Nicholas, I do care about you. I wish it weren't true, but it is."

That was the only response she felt she could give, the only one she thought he wanted to hear. "My darling," he whispered softly, leaning over and joining his lips with hers.

But the tender caress soon turned into an urgent need for both of them. As his hands pressed into the softness of her waist, eagerly stroking her warm skin, Thea felt a glow start in her abdomen, slowly growing hotter and hotter. She had never felt like this before, as if there were a fire burning in the center of her being, making her both excited and relaxed at the same time.

"Thea, I want you so badly." Nicholas' voice was shaking, and his breath had quickened.

The tremor in his voice made her even warmer. A feeling of heat was slowly melting her body, and she put her arms trustingly around his neck. His fingers moved under the soft material of her bikini top, teasing a nipple.

Nicholas stretched out next to her, his body molding into hers, and she felt his arousal. It was a satisfying feeling, and she trembled with pleasure at his touch.

"Thea, darling." His voice was even more urgent.

"Nicholas, I feel as though I'm suddenly coming alive." Thea nuzzled his neck with her nose, loving the texture of his skin, the warm sea scent of his body. Her tone was passionate, yet innocent, and the nuance wasn't lost on Nicholas. Suddenly the questions from two nights before flamed in his mind, and he knew he had to ask. Forcing himself to release her, he propped himself up on one elbow and looked down at her concerned face, now shadowed by his body.

"Thea . . ." Nicholas paused, unsure of how to phrase his words. "Thea, have you ever made love to a man?"

She looked up at him, startled, but instantly realized how important the question was. She had gotten lost in the wonderful wave of sensations they were creating in each other and had forgotten everything else.

She turned her head, trying to catch her breath. Then she answered him. "No, Nicholas, I haven't."

She felt him looking at her, and she met his gaze. She had thought he might be angry, but though a muscle twitched in his cheek his eyes were warm, loving.

"Your fiancé? . . ." He had to ask.

Thea sat up abruptly, absently brushing the sand

from her body. "We were engaged only a short time. I always wanted to wait . . . to share making love with the man I married. *When* I married. Robert respected my beliefs." She turned to him, trying to explain. "Besides, we weren't really sexually compatible. I mean, no lights went on in my head when he kissed me. But I really didn't know the difference. I had no one to compare him with."

Thea glanced at Nicholas. He was watching her intently, absorbing every word. It was several moments before he spoke. "And what would you have done today, now, if I hadn't stopped?"

"I don't know." Thea's words were honest. "I wasn't thinking. Like I said, I've never felt like this before. You make me feel so good that I just stop thinking and start feeling."

"I never would have started this if I had known." He sounded upset, and his brows had drawn together in a frown.

"Are you angry?" she asked softly.

"Not at you. Though you could have simplified matters by letting me know before things got out of hand."

"Were we that close?" The words popped out of Thea's mouth before she could think, and she blushed.

"Close enough." Nicholas was eyeing her ruefully, as if trying to come to a decision.

Thea felt herself flush again. "I'm sorry, Nicholas." She reached out to touch him, but he jerked away and she saw something akin to pain on his face. "Nicholas . . ."

He grabbed her hand even as he shied away, and the frustration he was feeling made him grip her wrist until she thought the bone would crack. "Thea, please . . . It's not that I don't want you to touch me. It's that I want you too much. Right now I'm at the edge of my self-control. Don't make it harder for me."

"I wasn't trying to. I didn't think." Her voice was barely a whisper.

The flat of his palm hit the sand, sending it flying in all directions. "I'm the one who didn't think. I should have known better. But I thought that since you had been engaged . . ." He trailed off helplessly, cursing his own stupidity.

"Believe me, I understand. I guess I'm a little different. Certainly most people would have made love if they'd been engaged. But I think I knew it was wrong from the beginning. The relationship with Robert, I mean. That made me even more cautious."

He looked at her, trying to make her understand. "Thea, you don't have to explain anything to me. I really understand, and I admire you for your views. I'm angry at myself."

"Don't be. Please." Thea looked at him, seeing how hard it was for him to stay in control. He was a virile, passionate man, and they had been on the verge of making love.

He looked down at his foot and kicked at the sand. His voice was low. "I meant what I said. I've never felt about any other woman as I feel about you. And I've never wanted a woman the way I want you."

"Nicholas." How she ached to reach out and touch him. She would give anything in the world to be able to tell him she loved him. But their situation was impossible. It would be cruel to tease him with her love.

"No, Thea, don't apologize. I'm the one who should be doing that. I let my own desires cloud my thinking. You're very special, you know." He was looking at her intently.

"No, I'm not." Thea was thrilled by his words, but she didn't really feel that she was unique. Many women held the same values.

"Yes, you are." His tone allowed no room for argument.

A seagull circled overhead and Thea looked up, trying to gather her thoughts. This was what she had feared, the intensity of their attraction causing them pain. Not only did they have the land sale between them, but now they were emotionally bonded. She was in love with him, but he hadn't mentioned a word about love. To desire her, to feel special about her didn't necessarily mean he loved her. Seeing him was only going to complicate things more and more.

"Nicholas," Thea ventured haltingly, "this is why I didn't want us to see each other again. Wouldn't it just be better to stop getting so close?"

"Don't say it!" his voice shot out like a whip. "It's crazy for us not to see each other. Feelings like these are too precious to waste."

But is it love for you, Nicholas? Thea wondered silently. If you haven't said the words, how can I know if you're feeling them? I love you, and the pain for me will be much worse before all this ends. But she kept the words to herself. Perhaps it would be better just to let the relationship take its course, and see what happened. She felt powerless to do anything right now, and she didn't believe Nicholas would leave her alone.

And she wanted to be with him. God, yes. Even now, she wanted to reach out and touch him, to stroke his head and wipe the pain from his eyes. Did he even suspect that she loved him? Did he realize that in trying to push him away, she was fighting for her own survival? She couldn't ask.

"Nicholas."

"Please, Thea, don't say that you won't see me again. I promise I won't let things get out of control."

She knew that she should stick to her guns and refuse to see him anymore, but she also knew that it would be impossible. To be on the same island with Nicholas, to be so close and not see him was unthinkable. Suddenly, she knew how the hapless sailors felt when they heard the Siren's song. She might be heading for the rocks, but she didn't care. She and Nicholas had a little time left. Soon life would separate them forever.

His voice cut into her thoughts. His breathing was still shaky, and Thea knew that his passion was only partly under control. "I apologize for my mistake,

Thea. But I don't apologize for wanting you. Do you understand?"

"Yes." Her voice was almost inaudible.

"Good. I'll try to keep things under control, but I insist on seeing you." There was a ragged, desperate quality to Nicholas' voice. He was on the edge of a precipice. Thea had no idea how alluring, how desirable she looked sitting there on the sand. Part of his mind was trying to think rationally, yet the other, more primitive half was urging him to take her in his arms, to caress the warm, salty flesh of her body. At the thought, he felt his loins grow hot, and his breathing became even shallower.

It would be so easy to take her, to convince her, he thought. In her innocence she had melted in his arms, trusting herself to his loving. He could do it again. But he knew he wouldn't try. He could stir her body to passion, but if she betrayed her values, she would have regrets. And more than anything in the world, he didn't want her to regret loving him.

A seagull cried overhead, its song both wild and plaintive. And in its call Nicholas and Thea both heard the pain and the joy of being alive. Nicholas covered Thea's hand with his, and they sat silently on the beach listening to the haunting music of the birds and the sea.

Chapter Seven

The rest of the week was bittersweet. Nicholas and Thea spent almost all of their free time exploring the island, swimming, sailing, or just relaxing quietly. They were both overwhelmed by their compatibility and the pleasure they experienced together. Thea's initial enthusiasm for sailing quickly turned to love, and Nicholas was a good teacher. They spent each morning out on the water, perfecting her skills. Then they would sit on the beach, swimming and sunbathing.

Both of them liked to read, and they would sit companionably on their blanket for hours, Thea lost in her novel, and Nicholas absorbed in the newspapers and trade magazines he devoured. Whenever he came across something he thought would interest her, he would pause and read it out loud. His taste ran from news articles about distant lands all the way to human interest stories.

To Thea's surprise, Nicholas liked to shop. At least, he liked to sightsee while she shopped. They returned to the marketplace several times so Thea could check on the merchandise she had wanted to order. Nicholas loved these sessions, though he was careful not to invade her territory. As she dickered with the manufacturers he would just listen, and he kept his comments to himself until they were alone.

At first she had been a little nervous about him observing her in action, but her apprehension disappeared after the first time he accompanied her. She was a pro at this aspect of her work, and she knew exactly what she was doing when she bargained for the best possible price. Nicholas smiled to himself as her face became animated and she absorbed herself in the details of the contracts. The men with whom she was dealing quickly grew to respect her ability, and the negotiations proceeded well.

"You're a shrewd horse trader," Nicholas said with admiration after she had successfully gotten the manufacturer of the sheepskin rugs to lower his price by one dollar per rug.

"Thank you." Thea's face was still pink from the pleasure she had felt at successfully closing the negotiations. "But I suppose it's to be expected. After all, half of my family came from this island and worked the marketplace. It must be in my genes."

Nicholas bent his head toward her face, his eyes teasing. "I certainly hope they weren't fishwives." They had just passed the fish market, and one particularly large and vocal fishwife had been waving a red snapper by the tail while yelling to potential buyers at the top of her voice. The scent of the fish had been overpowering.

"Very funny, Nicholas," Thea said acidly, pretending to be annoyed.

He put his arm around her affectionately, pulling her close, and his black eyes danced with laughter. "I can just see you waving a huge pompano around by the tail and yelling 'Best price, best price.'" He laughed uproariously at the thought. "The fish would probably outweigh you."

"In that case, I think I had better put on a few pounds. What about lunch?" Thea was trying hard not to laugh.

"Anything you say, my dear. Anything you say." Nicholas smiled, and something in his roguish look made Thea's pulse quicken. She turned her head, hoping that he hadn't noticed the effect he'd had on her. But it was futile. Nicholas noticed everything about her. His fingers teased the soft skin of her inner wrist as they walked up the hill, and she wondered if she would ever be able to hide a thing from this man.

Each night they took long strolls by themselves, reveling in the warm, dry weather. Invariably they would end up at the beach, and this was the part of the day that Thea and Nicholas both anticipated and dreaded. When they kept busy all day it was easier to keep the passion between them in check. Even when it surfaced they could distract themselves with something else, waiting for the intensity of their feelings to subside. But at night, on the warm, sandy beaches of Melinas, it was much more difficult to deny the undercurrent of desire coursing between them. In fact, it was almost impossible.

They would reach out to each other, eager for only one thing—to be in each other's arms. Nothing else seemed to matter. By day they were polite friends. At night, on the sand still hot from the Mediterranean sun, they were lovers, at last acknowledging the fires they had suppressed in the light of day.

True to his word, Nicholas didn't let things get totally out of hand, but Thea never knew how much strength that took from him. She saw the tightening of his jaw, the outward signs of establishing control, but she couldn't know the inner turmoil, the fire that consumed his body until he thought he would burn from the ache of unfulfilled longing and desire.

They would come together, unable to resist the teasing touch of their passion. But then they would draw away, both of them knowing that they should resist the ultimate temptation.

To Nicholas it was like being in heaven and hell all

at once. God, how he ached to take Thea into his arms, to teach her all there was to know about loving and love. But now that he understood her values, he would never let his own desires betray her trust in him. She never knew of the hours that he walked alone on the beach after he had taken her back to the hotel. In the moonlight he would imagine her soft body, naked and warm, and he swore he could smell the subtle perfume she favored. His senses on fire, he would pace back and forth on the sand, sometimes even shedding his clothes and swimming in the sea. At last, exhausted, he would finally return to his room at the hotel, only to fall into a troubled, frustrated sleep.

For Thea it was different. The fires he was kindling in her were teasing her to respond, to lose herself in him. She wanted to join with him. Yet, never having known the ultimate embrace, she was unable to pinpoint the sensation her body was tempting her to discover. Instead, she was consumed with a constant undercurrent of nervous energy, a wild desire to stay in motion and reach for something she couldn't quite identify. When she was in Nicholas' arms, she felt as if she were close. . . . And then they would draw apart, and she would experience a distinct feeling of loss.

And he never mentioned love. He cared for her, he desired her, he spent all his free time with her. Yet, he never said the words she wanted to hear. Carefully she examined her own emotions, and knew that she had been correct when she'd realized that she loved Nicholas. Every day the feeling grew stronger, and she came to accept it. But it was a silent acceptance. She would never put the burden of her love on Nicholas.

Besides their frustrated desire there was the ever-present problem of the land sale. They never discussed it, but it was an invisible wall that they both knew was there. John Prolisavis hadn't contacted either one of them, but it was only a matter of time. And then it would be over. One of them would have good reason to stay in Melinas. The other would not.

Thea tried to forget the problem as much as possible, and since she was so busy with Nicholas, it was easy to push thoughts of the land aside. But they stayed in a dark corner of her mind, and when she was alone she would think about it, trying to find a solution where there really was none.

The land became more difficult to forget on Friday morning. She and Nicholas met in the courtyard for breakfast. Thea had been happily anticipating yet another day of sailing and swimming when Nicholas' words broke into her thoughts.

"I have some things to do on my property today. Would you like to come with me?" His voice was easy, but Thea knew that he was waiting for her reaction.

Part of her wanted to say no. The land he already owned joined the property they were fighting over. But she was also curious to see just what he was doing. She toyed with the problem as she sipped her coffee.

Nicholas, sensing her unease, sat quietly, letting her work out the logistics in her mind. After a minute, Thea decided to go along. She wanted to see Nicholas' business, and by not going she was only pretending that their problem didn't exist.

"Sure," she answered lightly. "I'd love to see what you're doing."

"Good. We'll drive down in the Volvo. I think you'll find it interesting."

I bet I will, Thea thought ironically. But she kept silent. They quickly finished breakfast, and Nicholas assured her that her outfit, a blue cotton blouse with a matching peasant skirt, would be fine. They drove out of the village, and though they talked politely, both felt the tension increase between them.

The entrance road to Nicholas' property was about an eighth of a mile before Yaya's house. As Nicholas turned the Volvo down the dirt road leading to the sea Thea felt his excitement, and she couldn't suppress a smile. He was so proud of his venture.

And he had good reason to be. The Palmer Charter Boat Company was only half-complete, but with

Nicholas' explanations plus a view of the work already under construction, Thea got an excellent idea of what he was creating.

The focal point of the business centered around the dock area. Nicholas was building docking space to accommodate at least thirty boats. Ten of them, he informed her, would belong to him and would be rented out to tourists. The other spaces would be for privately owned yachts. The harbor of Melinas wasn't big enough to handle the influx of boats arriving each year.

He waved toward her grandmother's property, purposely keeping his voice businesslike. "The water over there is much deeper, so larger boats would be able to anchor with no problem. I figure that I would be able to dock at least ten fifty-footers in that location."

"You seem to have everything all planned out," Thea said, gritting her teeth. Her eyes were bright with anger.

"Of course. I'm a businessman." Nicholas gave her a sharp look, and saw the strained expression on her face. "I had to look at all aspects of the organization."

"All aspects except one!" Thea shot out. "You never planned on me!"

"That's true, but I certainly wish I had. Thea . . ." He gripped her shoulder, forcing her to look at him. "Believe me!"

Nicholas' face was like granite, but his arm pulled her close to his broad chest in an unbreakable grip.

"I do believe you. I know you're as innocent about this mess as I am, but it doesn't make it any easier." Thea's voice choked with unshed tears, and she tried to turn away. The anger which had flashed in her had died just as quickly, turning to sadness.

Knowing that she needed time to regain her self-control, Nicholas steered her gently toward several buildings that were under construction. They walked slowly, and after a few moments Thea trusted her voice enough to ask about the buildings.

Eagerly Nicholas explained, his enthusiasm showing clearly in his face. "When people come ashore, they need certain facilities, which I plan to provide. The small building to your right will be my office. From there I'll run the entire operation. With help, of course," he added. "The large building to your left will be an entertainment center. I plan to have an outdoor restaurant and bar. There will also be a small dress shop, and a general store to be stocked with boat supplies, food and other necessities. And there will be bathrooms and a shower area."

"Nicholas, this is amazing. It will be a wonderful success, I know it." Despite her frustration over their problems, Thea was genuinely impressed. He had a marvelous idea, and he was bringing it to fruition. The view was wonderful, and she could imagine people eager to rest in such a charming spot after days at sea. She thought for a moment.

"You know, you could add one more thing," she said consideringly.

"What?" Nicholas was eager to hear her idea. Thea was an excellent business woman.

"People arriving on their own boats will probably want to sightsee. You should provide some rental cars—have them at their disposal. It would be profitable, and it would be another lure to bring people here."

Nicholas considered the idea, then smiled in agreement. "Terrific. I'll have to look into it. It was something I overlooked."

"Well, sometimes two heads are better than one," Thea said casually, looking out over the water. She didn't see Nicholas' thoughtful look as he watched her.

Just then they were interrupted by a foreman who had a question for Nicholas. He excused himself and hurried off, and Thea had a few minutes to consider the entire operation. It certainly was a major project, and it was well under way. Nicholas had already invested a fortune in the place. Looking at it objectively, Thea realized how vital her land was to his venture. He would have a decent business without it, but with it, his idea would be a great commercial success. Did she really want to see his creation cut off at a crucial point? Was it fair to Nicholas that she win their battle, even if she possibly could?

But it was still *her* land! That was the way she thought about it, and she couldn't just discard a dream she had held for so long. Thea felt frustration and confusion gnaw at her, and, unbidden, her eyes filled again with tears.

She saw Nicholas approaching her, and she hurriedly wiped her eyes and put on her sunglasses.

"Thea, I'm really sorry, but they've run into a major problem with the construction. I'm going to be tied up for hours. Why don't you take the Volvo back to town? Do you mind?"

"Not at all," Thea assured him. She was more than ready to leave. "What time do you want me to pick you up?"

"Don't worry about me. Everyone here lives in the village. I'll get a ride with someone. I'll be busy till dusk, so take the car and enjoy yourself."

"Thanks a lot. I was thinking of visiting my cousin. Maybe I'll drive out to her villa."

"Great. Do anything you want, the tank's filled with gas." Nicholas walked Thea to the car, his hand holding hers tightly. "I'm really sorry about this. I wanted to spend the day with you."

"Don't worry about it. Things come up." Thea kissed him quickly and got into the driver's seat.

She had no problem with the automobile. She had once owned a Volvo. Carefully she navigated the car up the rocky dirt road and turned to the left. She had driven for only a minute when she saw the boundary stones marking her grandmother's land. Well, John Prolisavis' land. But to Thea it would always be her grandmother's property. She drew in a deep breath, subduing the familiar pain of frustration that the land now created within her, and firmly put the whole problem from her mind.

Forcing herself to concentrate on the treacherous,

winding road, Thea tried to recall the directions her cousin had given to her: five kilometers down from her grandmother's property, and a red mailbox to the right.

As Thea drove she couldn't help but enjoy the scenery. This road had an almost unobstructed view of the sea. In a few spots the road hugged the edge of the cliff, and there were no guardrails. The local people didn't seem to mind, but Thea gulped every time she came to such a spot. It would be so easy to drive right over the edge.

Finally, she arrived at the red mailbox and turned into the drive. Ahead lay a white stucco villa with an encircling patio. Behind the house, in all its glory, was the Ionian Sea.

Althea heard the car, and rushed out. "Thea, Thea, I thought you would never come to visit me," her cousin cried happily, kissing Thea on both cheeks.

"Of course I planned to visit, Allie." Thea smiled. She was truly glad to see her cousin.

"Let me show you around our home," Allie said, taking Thea by the arm. They entered the villa, and though it was hot outdoors, the cool stucco kept the inside temperature comfortable. There was a large living room with a picture window facing the sea, and four bedrooms. Allie was very proud of her two baths, and asked Thea anxiously if they were like the ones in America.

"Even better," Thea said, noticing that all the fixtures were made of white marble. In Greece marble was much less expensive than in America, and was used much more often.

Allie sighed, delighted with the news that her bathrooms were even nicer than those in America. She couldn't wait to tell her friends.

The house also boasted a modern kitchen, and there Allie introduced Thea to the local girl who helped out in the house. After Allie had pointed out every detail of her kitchen she drew Thea into the dining room, which also had an amazing view of the sea. Sliding glass windows led out to the patio.

Flowers were everywhere, vying for space with the wicker furniture.

They settled down comfortably, and the hired girl brought out tall glasses of vasinatha, a sweet drink made of cherries and syrup, and a plate of Greek cookies.

"So what have you been doing with yourself?" Allie asked, taking a bite of a large sweet pastry filled with sugared almonds.

"Nothing much," Thea said evasively, trying not to meet Allie's eyes.

"Is that what they call romance in America— nothing much?" Allie laughed. She looked like a plump little bird, merrily teasing her cousin.

Thea met her cousin's amused stare with an astonished look. How did Allie know about her and Nicholas?

"The island grapevine is very accurate." Allie smiled, reading her thoughts. "My husband's cousin works at the hotel, and my best friend cooks at one of the village tavernas. I passed you both the other day, but you didn't see me, though I honked my horn as a crazy."

"Like crazy," Thea corrected automatically, feeling both irritated and amused. Evidently there were no secrets on this island. "Was that you who almost ran us over?"

"Yes. I mean, no, I didn't almost run you over. I was just trying to get your attention." Allie was a little indignant.

"Well, you certainly succeeded. We were running for our lives."

Allie raised her dark eyebrows expressively, "It is hard to run, yes, when you have your arms wrapped around each other?" She had come to the point with Mediterranean clarity. No beating around the bush.

Thea couldn't hide the troubled expression crossing her face. She was just too drained. She looked at her cousin, her blue eyes filling with tears.

"Thea." Allie's voice reflected her concern. "It cannot be so bad!"

"Yes, it can!" Thea moved uncomfortably.

"Because you love him?" Again Allie went right to the heart of the matter.

"Is it so obvious?" Thea's voice was bleak.

"To me it is." Allie reached out and took her cousin's hand and gave it a comforting squeeze. "But I really don't understand what the problem is. What is so wrong with being in love? Isn't it time you settled down?"

"Oh, Allie," Thea whispered, tears constricting her throat. "The problem is that *he* doesn't love *me*." Although she hadn't planned to confide in her cousin, she couldn't help it. She needed the release of talking to another woman. The words came flooding out, and slowly Allie was able to picture the entire situation. When Thea finally finished, Allie sat silently for a moment, digesting the facts.

Then she looked up at Thea, her brown eyes twinkling. "You know, Thea, I read somewhere that love is blind, and I think this is true in more ways than one. I'm sure Nicholas loves you. He wouldn't want to be with you all the time if he didn't."

Thea shrugged, discounting her cousin's theory. "He likes me a lot, cares about me, but that isn't love."

"Are you so sure?" Allie was firm.

For one moment Thea allowed hope to flare in her heart, but she quickly suppressed it. Another thought had come to mind. "Allie, even if he loves me, it still doesn't solve the situation. One of us will get the land and the other won't. Period."

Allie didn't answer. Thea had a point. This was a complex situation. Allie's warm face clouded with worry as she considered her cousin's dilemma. She was one of those people who loved to make things right for those she cared about, but now she could think of little which would truly help Thea.

Thea shook her head as if to signal the end of that part of the conversation. "Well, at least you know how things stand. Have you heard from John?"

"Not since I last spoke to you. But he did say it

would be a full ten days until we heard his decision. We know he would definitely prefer to sell to you. His mother and your grandmother were girlhood friends."

"I appreciate all you've done. Both you and Dimitri."

"Don't even talk about it," Allie exclaimed. "Who can you turn to for help, if not family?"

Thea smiled ruefully. "Well, I do thank you anyway. Unfortunately, in the end I don't think that John will be able to turn down Nicholas' open-ended bid for the land."

Allie shrugged her shoulders, conveying her whole philosophy of life. "Don't be so sure, Thea. Life can play strange tricks. You've read the Greek myths. You know that the strangest twists of fate can alter things beyond our wildest expectations."

"Those are myths, Allie. Stories."

"No, Thea. Myths are life in a . . ." Allie hesitated, groping for the right word. "Life in a nutshell, as you Americans say. You never know what might change your fate." Allie's tone left no room for argument.

Thea laughed. "Well, speaking of myths, I was planning to visit the temple of Diana this afternoon. Can you give me directions?"

"Oh, you'll love it." Quickly Allie drew a map showing Thea how to find the temple. "But be careful. The road is narrow, and not too good."

Thea readily agreed to exercise caution, and after a few minutes took leave of her cousin and headed for the car. She consulted the map again. It certainly wasn't a long drive. Only about five miles from Allie's villa.

But as she drove to the site, Thea realized that Allie had been right. This road was even worse than the other one. Deep potholes pitted the ground, reminding Thea of small craters. At one particularly treacherous spot, the road bordered a cliff dropping to the sea, and, on its other side a deep ravine plunged fifty feet to an olive grove below. Thea concentrated so carefully on her driving that she almost missed the entrance to the archeological site, and turned the Volvo just in time.

The narrow dirt road led down to the beach, where a makeshift parking lot had been set up. As she parked the car, Thea looked out on the Ionian Sea, remembering the day she and Nicholas had sailed past here. What a perfect day that had been!

She walked across the sand to the entrance of the cave and read the sign. There was a token admission charge, and the site was open until dusk. Archeological crews were working inside, and tourists were asked to abide by any instructions they might give.

Thea paid the admission to a young woman who was sitting in the entrance to the cave, and she was given a brochure written in Greek, French, and English. She quickly scanned it. The first room of the cave was the shrine of St. Constantina.

Thea entered the cave and let her eyes adjust for a moment from the bright sunlight. Candles burned in sconces shedding just enough light to see, but gradually Thea's eyes adjusted and she began to look around with real interest. The brochure said that this was the room where Constantina had hidden the children of Melinas the day the Moslems attacked the island. Looking around the sides of the shrine, Thea saw beautiful murals on the walls. Hordes of medieval warriors were depicted landing on Melinas, while further down a fragile woman in blue was herding children into the cave by the sea.

Thea moved down the length of the cave, reading the picture story. The next mural showed Constantina being taken prisoner, and the third showed her being executed, while in the background the children could be seen still safely hidden in the cave.

On the opposite wall was a magnificent mural of Constantina in heaven, surrounded by other saints and religious figures. It was done in the Byzantine style favored by the Greek Orthodox Church. The halos around the saints were composed of gold leaf, while the colors used were vivid blues, greens, and reds. The far end of the room contained an altar covered with a plain white cloth, and behind it stood a Byzantine cross of gold.

In the back of the shrine was a cedar door, and Thea pushed it open. It led to the second room of the cave, and though this room contained electric lights, this modern touch did little to invade the ancient darkness of the inner sanctuary. She was in the ancient temple of Diana.

Thea shivered at the realization. The gray stone walls soared upward, finally disappearing into the hovering darkness. The lights were only a token concession to the twentieth century. As Thea looked around she knew that she had stepped back in time to antiquity.

She heard a slight movement, and realized that four people were working in the back of the cave, carefully sifting through the soft earth. They were archeologists, Thea knew immediately. She was the only tourist.

Thea had read the brochure and knew that the ancient temple had been discovered four years earlier when the Greek Orthodox Church decided to turn the cave into a shrine to St. Constantina. During their building project, they began to uncover artifacts dating to the time before Christ. They called in a team of archeologists from the University of Athens. The experts quickly realized that they had a great historical find, and work had commenced in earnest three years ago.

Thea looked around the temple, trying to decide what to examine first. The ancient altar to the goddess had been uncovered and was standing in all its glory against the stone walls of the cave. It was made of white marble with a gold vein running through it, and the marble shimmered like a pearl in the night.

In front of the altar was a magnificent mosaic floor set carefully into the hard ground. Thea studied it with fascination, marveling at the skill of the ancient craftsmen who had labored so lovingly before the altar of the goddess they worshipped. The mosaic stones consisted of such vivid colors that two thousand years had not dimmed their beauty. The blue was the exact color of the sea, and the white was the shade of sea foam when it touched the beach.

But the most magnificent part of the mosaic was its center. Perfectly formed, as if from some divine hand, was an enormous golden rose, appearing to hover over blue water as if cast there by the hand of the goddess. The rose was made of gold mosaic, fashioned to flow perfectly into the shape the ancient craftsmen desired. It gave off a glow that seemed almost supernatural, and Thea held her breath, feeling as though she were in the presence of something not of this world.

It was only after several minutes had elapsed that she could force herself to turn to the other parts of the mosaic, which depicted the tale of Diana and her lover. These were also done with a simplicity and clarity which told the tale beautifully without words. In one small panel, Diana and her prince embraced, clinging to each other in the way of lovers. At their feet lay Melinas, the land they both ruled.

In the next square, an angry Zeus, king of all the gods and goddesses, stood between Diana and her lover, keeping them apart with thunderbolts. Diana was on her knees, her shining hair cascading around her naked hips as she pleaded with Zeus for the life of her lover. A third panel showed ethereal spirits dragging the sobbing Diana away as her lover held the empty crown of Melinas in his hand. His look was sorrowful and lost.

Thea looked toward the final part of the mosaic, transfixed with awe. In this panel, the background was a midnight blue sky lit only by a perfect full moon, the symbol of Diana. And hurling out of the sky like a comet was the golden rose, an exact replica of the one in the center. It contained such energy, such urgency, that Thea almost believed she could see the magic hand of the goddess behind it: Diana rushing to earth to meet her lover!

Thea held her breath, afraid to move, fearing it

would break the spell. She suddenly understood Diana, could feel her joy and pain, her love and her sorrow.

"It's pretty incredible, isn't it?" said a voice behind her, and Thea jumped, turning quickly. One of the archeologists was standing to her left, watching her reaction with amusement.

Thea laughed. "It certainly is. I felt like I was drifting back in time. I almost thought I could see Diana arriving."

The young man nodded in agreement. "Almost everyone has the same reaction," he said in perfect English. His voice held only a trace of a Greek accent. "The workmanship is so good that it transports you into another world."

"Like all great works of art," Thea said.

"Yes," the young man agreed. "Diana was greatly beloved by the ancient Greeks. Their greatest artists and craftsmen vied with each other to produce the most wonderful works of art depicting their goddess."

"They certainly excelled in this temple," Thea murmured, her gaze moving to the golden rose on the mosaic floor. She could have sworn she saw a petal move slightly in the quiet room.

"Let me show you some of the smaller mosaics we've uncovered." The young man was eager to guide her around the site. He now motioned to a darker section of the cave.

"Diana was the goddess of the hunt and the moon," the archeologist explained, pointing to a mosaic of a moon in all its stages: new, half, three-quarter, and full. Next to it was a mosaic of Diana, this time in a short tunic, holding a bow in one hand and a spear in the other. On her back was a brace of arrows. She looked quite ferocious, and Thea thought about the two sides of the goddess: one a lover, the other queen of the hunt. She mentioned this to the archeologist.

"That's true, and that's the reason why the legend of the golden rose is so poignant. Diana was the huntress, and she loved to win. The sacrifice she made for her lover was all the greater because it went against her nature."

Thea thoughtfully considered the idea, and then felt a slight ache of pain in her chest. Somehow, the young man's words were hitting too close to home. The archeologist didn't notice her sudden silence, however, and he continued with his tour of the little temple.

The archeologist was knowledgeable and Thea spoke with him for almost two hours. She was amazed when one of his colleagues announced that it was quitting time. Sadly she left the temple and re-entered the shrine of St. Constantina.

After pausing in front of the altar and saying a brief prayer, she walked outside. It was almost seven o'clock now, and the sun was beginning to sink into the horizon, though it would be daylight for almost another hour. The wind from the sea was refreshing after the warm, heavy incense, and Thea inhaled the fresh air deeply.

It was so beautiful outside, and so peaceful. When the archeological crew came out and headed for their cars, she decided to linger on the beach for a while. She cheerfully declined their offers to give her a ride, pointing to the red Volvo.

Although the beach was totally deserted, she felt perfectly safe. Violent crimes were almost entirely unknown in Melinas, and she knew that she could enjoy a few moments of solitude undisturbed. And that was exactly what she needed, she decided as she sat down on the warm sand. She needed to be alone to think.

As she listened to the gentle lap of the waves, her mind reviewed all that she had seen today. Both Constantina and Diana had made sacrifices to save the ones they loved. Diana had given up Melinas to save her lover, and Constantina had given her life for the children of the island. Thea couldn't help but make parallels with her own predicament.

The dilemma she had struggled with earlier in the day came back with new urgency. Should she give up her claim on Yaya's property and leave Melinas? Would that be the right thing to do? She had no idea. She had hoped that the peace and solitude of the deserted beach would help clear her mind, but once again she was disappointed. There was still no answer to the question which plagued her, and finally she sighed in frustration and gave up trying to figure things out.

Miserably she stared out to sea, trying to let the eternal serenity of the water calm her spirit. Slowly she began to relax, soothed by the continual pattern of the waves coming onto the beach. Like little beacons the stars began to appear, and the moon rose, replacing the sun in the evening sky. Diana's moon. It would be another year before the goddess could return to earth to visit her lover, Thea thought sadly.

Finally she rose, dusting the sand from her clothes. Even though she hated to leave this quiet spot, she knew she should be heading into town. Nicholas would be worried if she were too late.

Nicholas. At the thought of him, her heart gave its usual little flutter, and, even now, with all her troubles, Thea knew that she was eager to see him.

Actually, eager was a mild description for the way she suddenly felt. All at once the peace and quiet of the empty beach became too lonely, and she wanted to be with Nicholas. She wanted to see his inviting smile, and feel the warmth of his mouth when he kissed her hello.

Thea couldn't wait to get back to town. She got into the Volvo and flipped on the headlights. It was darker than she'd realized; her eyes had been adjusting to the gradually dimming light on the beach. She glanced at the car clock, and saw that it was almost seven-thirty. With a little luck, she would be back at the village by eight.

Chapter Eight

Thea underestimated the time it would take to return to the village. Night was rapidly approaching, and she had forgotten the terrible road conditions. She was forced to slow down to a crawl to navigate the treacherous potholes on the twisting, turning highway safely. When she came to the first bend overlooking the sea, she felt the hair on her neck rise. A single error in judgment could send her plunging over the cliff to the water below.

"Damn, why did I stay so late?" she muttered to herself. I should have remembered how bad the road was, especially this part. Even though she had enjoyed the solitude of the lonely beach, it still wasn't worth this night drive back to the village.

She tried to recall the highway as it appeared in the daylight. There had been three dangerous spots, she remembered. A few minutes later she was on the second turn, and then on the third. It was only after she had cleared the third cliff that she allowed herself to relax slightly, and realized that she had been holding the steering wheel in a white-knuckled grip.

A few minutes later her slow pace came to a dead halt. She had reached a cluster of tiny cottages, and a shepherd was bringing his lambs home for the night. The prancing animals had blocked the entire road. Thea stopped the car and waited. Though she was a trifle exasperated at the delay, she couldn't help but smile at the antics of the lambs. One curious ewe came right to the side of the car, and Thea opened the window and patted the friendly animal on the head.

Once the delay was over, she started the Volvo and headed south. By now it was completely dark, but Thea was more relaxed, and this part of the road didn't seem as treacherous.

Perhaps that was the reason she wasn't prepared for the oncoming car that tore out of the darkness ahead. She had just navigated a sharp curve when the sudden appearance of the car startled, then frightened her. The other car passed too widely, forcing Thea onto the shoulder, then disappeared around the curve, its driver unaware that Thea had gone into a screeching skid.

Thea struggled to get the Volvo back in the lane, but the road twisted again and before she knew what was happening the car slid down a steep embankment, crashing through the brush until it finally came to rest against an olive tree. One headlight was knocked out, the other continued to shine.

The impact threw Thea against the driver's door, and she felt a sickening flash of pain tear through several parts of her body. Her head hit the steering wheel, but she wasn't knocked unconscious. She was only dazed.

It took her a few minutes to get her bearings, and she slowly realized that she was hurt. She reached out a hand and gingerly felt her forehead, wincing as she touched the lump on her head. Then she tried to lift herself away from the door, but an excruciating pain made her gasp and she sank back, her breathing ragged.

I've broken my arm or my shoulder, she thought as tears of pain rolled down her cheeks. She sat there for a few minutes, willing the agony to subside, then tried to think of what to do. If a broken arm was the extent of her injuries, perhaps she could open the door with her other hand, and climb up to the road. She would have a better chance of being found up there than down in the ravine.

But this proved to be impossible. When she tried to shift her legs, another fiery pain racked her body and she realized that she had seriously injured her knee. She didn't know if it was broken, but she knew that she would never be able to climb the steep hill. She was trapped in the car.

Thea had read about automobile accidents, but she had never been in one and now she realized how terrifying it was. Especially since she was all alone. She tried to fight down the panic which was rising in her, and after a few moments she felt it subside, only to be replaced by a feeling of total helplessness.

She knew that she wasn't critically hurt, but she *was* injured badly enough that she wouldn't be able to move from the car. And it could be hours before they found her. When did Nicholas say he would return? She tried to remember, fighting the throbbing pain in her head. He had said that he would return after they solved the problem at the dock. He had probably decided that she'd just stayed late at her cousin's house. In that case, he wouldn't become concerned until ten or eleven o'clock. Then it could take hours to find her. It might even take until morning.

Helplessness turned to despair as the pain from her injuries began to increase. Thea felt as if every nerve in her body was aching. Movement added to the pain, so she forced herself to stay absolutely still. Slowly, her body began to respond with its normal defense mechanisms and she began to get sleepy. After a few minutes, she slipped from consciousness with a small sigh.

In fact, Nicholas was back at the hotel at five, relieved that the problem with the construction had been successfully solved. After discovering that Thea had not returned, he assumed she'd decided to have dinner with Allie, so he took a shower, and changed his clothes. Then, with reluctance, he headed for a taverna to eat alone, totally oblivious to the admiring glances cast his way by the single women in the plaza.

It was a dismal meal. He missed Thea. It was amazing how much a part of his life she had become in such a short period of time. Supper without her was boring and lonely, and he found himself looking up constantly to see if she had returned.

And besides just missing her, he wanted to talk to her about this afternoon. Her distress about the land certainly had not escaped him. All day long he had been plagued by the memory of her face when she had become upset at him. They had to talk about it.

Like Thea, Nicholas had been able to block out the problem of the land dispute when they were together. But today at the construction site, he had been forced to face the barrier which divided them, and it hit home with painful clarity. He knew that it would hurt Thea terribly to lose the property, and he couldn't bear to think of her unhappiness. He was even tempted to withdraw his bid. Yet, the land was vital to his business.

He would have to make some important decisions soon, he decided.

But before he could think about it any further, a worker from the site joined him and they began talking about business. Nicholas was almost glad he had someone to distract him from his jumbled thoughts. When he glanced at his watch, it was almost eight o'clock, and he decided that Thea must be back at the hotel. He'd go find her, and they could go out for a drink. His mood immediately brightened at the idea.

He felt a moment's unease when he found that she hadn't returned to the hotel, but he told himself he was being foolish. He had said he might not be back until dusk, and night had just fallen. She would probably be back within the hour.

Feeling restless, Nicholas went for a short walk, but

he kept searching the road for the red Volvo. He finally abandoned his pacing and returned to the hotel. A drink at the bar tasted flat and, instead of relaxing him, only made him feel more restless.

His unease grew as the minutes passed, and with his greater unease came frustration, and finally fear. He knew that the road to her cousin's house was bad, and he started to imagine all sorts of horrible things. And he didn't have a car to use to go look for her.

But Nicholas was a man who had faced many crises, and though he was upset, he forced himself to be cool and think logically. The first thing to do was to call her cousin. But what was Allie's last name? He didn't know. However, he did know where she lived. Thea had told him.

To get to Allie's house he would need a car. Nicholas thought for a moment, knowing that the rental agency would be closed. Then the pirate in him took over. His concern for Thea overrode any other consideration. He would commandeer a car. If necessary, he would even steal one.

Nicholas strode into the courtyard and collared a young waiter whom he knew owned a car. In short, terse sentences he explained his problem, and handed the waiter fifty dollars. The young man, John, waved the money aside and gave Nicholas the keys. Of course a man should go look for his woman! In fact, he would come, too. He knew the area very well.

Nicholas agreed that it would be a big help. John rushed off to tell his boss, and the two men strode out of the hotel and over to the waiter's tiny Datsun. Nicholas insisted on driving and John didn't argue. He realized that the American needed to be in control.

Nicholas forced himself to drive at a decent speed, but only because he and the young Greek were carefully examining the road for signs of the Volvo. The waiter knew Thea's cousin, and he gave helpful directions as they drove. John prayed that nothing had happened to the young woman. He didn't want to think about what this Mr. Palmer might do if something were really wrong.

When they reached the red mailbox signaling Allie's home, Nicholas breathed a sigh of relief. She had to be there. They hadn't passed anyone on the lonely beach road, and there had been no signs of a wreck. But his relief was short-lived when he saw that the driveway contained only a green pickup truck.

Allie and her husband had heard the car, and they rushed out to greet their visitors. But when Allie saw Nicholas, she felt her heart sink in fear.

"Thea?" she cried, realizing at once that something terrible must have happened.

"Isn't she here?" Nicholas demanded, his own fear making him speak abruptly.

"This afternoon she was here," Allie whispered. "But she went to visit the temple of Diana."

"I know where it is!" John cried.

"Let's go." Nicholas jumped back into the Datsun, trying not to think the worst.

"We'll follow you," Allie yelled after them. She and her husband Dimitri hurried to start the pickup truck, and then did their best to keep up with the Datsun careening down the road.

Nicholas felt fear gnaw at his belly. Now he knew for sure that something was terribly wrong. The archeological site closed at dusk, and it was almost eleven o'clock now. Could there have been a cave-in, a freak flood? As he conjured up the worst horrors, he cursed himself unmercifully for waiting so long before trying to find her.

John felt Nicholas' fear, and suggested another possibility: Perhaps Thea had had car trouble and was just sitting patiently waiting in the Volvo until help arrived. It was a comforting thought, but it was dashed when they made a turn around a sharp bend.

It was the waiter who cried out. "Over there! A light!"

Nicholas slammed on the brakes and brought the protesting Datsun to a halt. He leaped from the vehicle and started to run down the ravine, his eyes never leaving the Volvo, which was resting against a gnarled olive tree, one headlight shining with a ghostly light.

As Nicholas raced down the hill, tripping over cascading rocks and dirt, he prayed as he had never prayed before in his life. "Please, God, let her be all right," he said over and over.

But when he peered into the window of the Volvo, his worst fears were confirmed. Looking at Thea's limp form trapped between the door and the steering wheel, he knew that she was either dead or unconscious, and his heart stopped beating in his chest. Then he pulled the door open, and Thea turned, waking from her half-conscious sleep, and Nicholas felt a surge of relief race through his body.

"Nicholas." She murmured, trying to smile. She was overcome with relief and happiness at seeing him at last.

"Thea, my God. Thank God!" He wanted to crush her in his arms, to hold her tight, but he knew how foolish that would be.

"I knew you would come," Thea whispered softly, her eyes trying to focus on his face. It was so good to hear his voice. She suddenly felt safe and secure.

"I wish I had been with you . . . I wish I hadn't let you go ahead without me." Nicholas said hoarsely.

"It was my fault. Another car spooked me on the turn and I went off the shoulder. Lucky it wasn't the cliff."

"Damn lucky," Nicholas agreed fervently. He studied her carefully, trying to assess her injuries. "Do you know how badly you're hurt?" he asked, wiping the blood from her forehead. She had a bruise the size of a robin's egg forming above her right eye.

Thea winced, and tried to move her head away. "Something's wrong with my left shoulder, and my right knee. I think both may be broken. And I hit my head on the steering wheel."

"Are you having any difficulty breathing?" Nicholas was thinking of broken ribs, possibly a pierced lung.

"No." Thea was trying to remember. "I think the

part of my body which took the brunt of the impact was my left shoulder. I braked when I went down into the ravine, and I wasn't going too fast to start with. My knee swung up under the dashboard, and that's how it got hurt. But I don't think I have any internal injuries."

Nicholas frowned as he knelt by the side of the car. He could see Thea shivering, though the night was warm, and he knew that she had to see a doctor immediately. He turned to John, who was hovering behind him, and asked about the ambulance situation on Melinas.

John shook his head with regret. There wasn't one. And no hospital, either. The young man blanched at the curses Nicholas uttered when he received this piece of news.

Just then Allie and Dimitri reached them, and Nicholas quickly assured them that Thea's injuries didn't appear to be critical. But she did need a doctor immediately. He thought for a moment, and then made his decision. He told them in a few brief sentences what he intended to do, his eyes never leaving Thea's face.

Allie and John would drive on ahead and get the doctor, and bring him to Allie's house. Nicholas would carry Thea to the pickup truck and ride with her in the back. Dimitri would drive the truck. They all agreed on the plan, and Allie and John hurried away while Nicholas explained everything again to Thea.

"I'm afraid it's really going to hurt when I lift you out," Nicholas said, but Thea agreed it had to be done.

"Don't listen to me if I scream," Thea said, meaning it as a joke. But Nicholas winced at her words and berated himself again for waiting so long to find her. When he lifted her from the wreck, she couldn't suppress the moans of pain that tore through her body, and his heart cried out at her suffering.

Once Thea was out of the car, Nicholas laid her on the ground, then picked her up again as gently as

possible, shifting her small weight against his strong
body in the way that seemed the most comfortable for
her. The trip up the hill was slow because he didn't
want to joggle her, and he also feared slipping on the
treacherous, rocky ground.

It took them almost half an hour to reach the truck.
Dimitri had laid a blanket on the cold metal surface,
and Nicholas carefully arranged Thea on it. She was
only half-conscious again. The pain in her shoulder
and knee had made her faint.

"Drive slowly," Nicholas commanded. "I want her
to be jostled as little as possible."

Dimitri nodded in agreement, and Nicholas settled
down next to Thea, resting her head in his lap, and
took her cold hand in his. Slowly the pickup truck
began to move down the narrow, twisting road.

Later, Thea would have only the vaguest memory
of the ride. She was aware of only two things: the pain
which seemed to consume her entire body, and the
feel of Nicholas' warm hand holding hers securely.
Without understanding she heard his comforting
words of encouragement, but all she needed was the
sound of his voice to make her feel that everything
would be all right.

For Nicholas it was a ride he would remember for
the rest of his life, especially in his nightmares. He felt
so helpless watching Thea suffer; he would have given
anything to take the pain and bear it himself. When
she moaned and tightened her fingers around his
hand, he felt tears come to his eyes, and he cursed
himself all over again.

He watched her pale face, lit only by the moonlight,
and he prayed that her injuries weren't critical. She
didn't appear to have any serious internal or head
injuries, but one could never tell. And he cursed the
island again for not having an ambulance or a hospital. If necessary, he would charter a plane and take
her to Athens, he decided.

It seemed like an eternity later when they finally
arrived at Dimitri's house. Allie was waiting outside,

and with her was the doctor, who had brought a stretcher. He and Nicholas carried Thea into the house to one of the bedrooms.

Nicholas wanted to stay while they examined her, but the doctor was firm. He ordered Nicholas outside, and he and Allie began the examination.

Nicholas fumed outside the bedroom door, and John and Dimitri retreated to the dining room after he brusquely declined a glass of ouzo. Understanding his fear, they left him alone to pace back and forth like a caged animal.

After about twenty minutes the door opened, and Nicholas practically grabbed the doctor by the throat. "Well?"

"Relax, Mr. Palmer. She is in much better shape than we originally imagined." The doctor closed the door and smiled. "There is no concussion or internal injuries. She has a dislocated shoulder, and a twisted right knee. I've taped both. And she has a good lump on the head, but it is more painful than serious."

"Do you think we should take her to the mainland?" Nicholas demanded, hardly daring to breath a sigh of relief.

"No. I don't think it is necessary. I've done all that can be done. And I've given her a painkiller. By the way, she should rest for at least a week, preferably in bed. Even less serious injuries than hers take a toll on the body."

"Of course, of course," Nicholas agreed. "Can I see her?"

"Certainly, though the painkiller will soon start taking effect. She'll be going to sleep, so don't stay too long."

Nicholas rushed into the bedroom. Allie was just arranging a quilt over Thea, and she smiled at him. "Praise God, it isn't too bad," she whispered.

Nicholas didn't even hear her. He pulled a chair next to the bed and took Thea's hand in his. Her eyelids fluttered at his touch, recognizing the familiar warmth of his hand.

"Nicholas," she whispered, marveling at the soft, calm feeling overcoming her. She wondered if it was the painkiller.

"Thea, you're going to be all right." Nicholas' voice was both relieved and strained. Even though he knew that her injuries weren't serious, she still looked terrible with that big bruise on her forehead. He ached to touch her lovingly, yet knew she should stay still.

"I wrecked your car," she whispered, concern suddenly overcoming the sedative. Her eyes flickered open and searched for his.

"Don't be silly." Nicholas would gladly have smashed ten cars if it would save Thea from hurt. "The doctor says you have to rest for at least a week."

"Will you come and see me?" she asked, fighting off the sleep that was becoming overwhelming. She didn't want to miss being with Nicholas.

"Try and keep me away," he growled, furious even at the idea. He saw her eyelids quiver, then close, though a faint smile stayed on her lips. In a moment her breathing became deep and regular, and he knew she had fallen asleep.

But he couldn't tear himself away from her just yet. Gently he reached out and pushed back a strand of copper hair slightly damp from perspiration. He settled it into place, and then stroked her cheek, careful not to disturb her. She looked so young and vulnerable lying there. What would he have done if she had been killed? The thought was so painful that he couldn't even examine it. With a shudder he thrust the idea out of his mind. She was all right, and that was that. He said a silent prayer of thanksgiving.

When Allie looked in a while later, he was still sitting by the bed holding Thea's hand, and Allie closed the door softly, not wanting to disturb him. It was almost one in the morning before Nicholas appeared. Allie, Dimitri, and John were sitting in the living room sipping wine.

"She is sleeping, yes?" Allie asked. The doctor had reassured her that Thea's injuries were minimal, and she was not too worried. However, she looked at Mr. Palmer with real interest. Now that everything had calmed down, she remembered how upset he had been about Thea. Actually, upset was too mild a word. He had been sick with worry. To Allie this confirmed her original theory that Mr. Palmer loved Thea. Perhaps the accident would have some redeeming value—the gods played strange tricks to reach their goals.

Allie smiled with real warmth, and offered Nicholas a seat. He sank into the soft cream-colored sofa with a sigh of weariness, and gladly accepted the glass of wine Allie handed him. He felt drained.

"I want to thank you very much for your help," he said, including everyone in his thanks. "I don't know what I would have done without all of you."

"Don't mention it, Nicholas," Dimitri said. "After all, isn't Thea my wife's cousin?" Dimitri was a pleasant-looking man with a receding hairline who looked amazingly like his wife.

"Still . . ." Nicholas was too exhausted to frame his words.

"No still!" Allie said firmly, refilling his wineglass. "Let's all just be thankful she will be fine."

"Will it be any problem for you to take care of her? I can have a nurse sent by," Nicholas suggested, eager to do anything he could. He didn't see Allie smile at his possessive tone. Clearly he thought of Thea as his responsibility.

"I'll have no problem at all," Allie assured him. "I have a girl who comes in each day to help. It will be a delight to take care of Thea. I can talk to her all day long."

"Which, I assure you, she will do," Dimitri said, rolling his eyes toward the ceiling.

Everyone laughed. Then John stood, eager to go home.

"Just one second," said Nicholas quickly. "I just want to check on Thea." He went back into the bedroom, and closed the door. Allie smiled at her husband. Things were working out quite well.

Chapter Nine

Thea awoke the next morning feeling groggy and confused. As she drifted from sleep to alertness, she could hear the distant sound of waves, and she tried to figure out where she was. There were no waves in Manhattan! She opened her blue eyes, and looked around the sunny, unfamiliar room, and experienced a moment of sheer panic before memory came flooding back.

She shifted her body slightly, and pain flashed through her left arm. Immediately she stopped moving and tried to recall what the doctor had said. A dislocated left shoulder and a twisted knee. She raised her right arm gingerly and felt her forehead. And a good-sized lump on her head.

Trying to tell herself that she was lucky, she rested back against the pillows. My God, I destroyed Nicholas' car, she thought with a sick feeling. Of course, it was only a rental and it was insured, but still . . . Thea cursed herself for having left the archeological site so late. If it had been lighter, she would never have been spooked by the other car.

She closed her eyes, trying to remember what else the doctor had said. She had to stay in bed for a week! Thea groaned out loud at the dismal thought. What a terrible way to spend the rest of her vacation. She had so much she wanted to do. She couldn't possibly play invalid for so long. She wouldn't!

Forcing herself to sit up, Thea suppressed the pain that set every nerve on edge and tried to swing her legs over the side of the bed. She moved slowly, intent on making her actions as painless as possible. She was so absorbed that she didn't hear Allie enter the room.

"Just what do you think you are doing?" her cousin cried indignantly. Allie stood in the doorway, her hands on her plump hips, an outraged expression on her usually placid face.

"Getting out of bed," Thea said, gritting her teeth. She was using all her willpower to keep moving.

"Only to go to the bathroom," Allie declared firmly. "The doctor said you should spend the next week in bed. Or, at least, the next few days. Then you can sit outside for a while each day."

"Allie, I can't spend the week in bed," Thea wailed.

"Why not?" Allie was blunt.

"Because." Thea was just as stubborn. She was not going to stay in bed. "Can you at least help me to the bathroom?"

Allie had raised three children, and she knew how to handle this situation. Disapprovingly she helped Thea to the large marble bath, then waited outside. When Thea finally came out, Allie knew she had won. Thea's face was pale, and a thin line of sweat covered her upper lip. There was no way she could move around today. With a sigh of defeat, Thea allowed Allie to help her back to bed, ignoring her cousin's satisfied smirk.

After Allie plumped up the pillows she left the room, and Thea lay back gratefully, allowing herself a little moan of relief. She felt as if every part of her body was bruised. And the shock of seeing her face in the mirror had almost made her ill. The bump on her forehead was so large that she looked like she had an egg under her skin. And it was turning red, blue, and orange.

What would Nicholas think when he saw her? she wondered. She looked as glamorous as an omelet.

Just then Allie returned with a black ceramic tray. On it rested a white china coffeepot, a plate of crisp rolls, and a chilled glass of orange juice. "The doctor said to eat lightly today," she explained, not guessing that this was Thea's normal breakfast.

"Allie, I look terrible," Thea cried morosely, taking another glance at the hand mirror on the table beside the bed. "What will Nicholas think when he sees me?"

"I didn't ask him," Allie answered with amusement, pulling up a chair.

Thea looked up in surprise. "Was he here already?" She felt her heart sink in disappointment. She had missed him.

"He was here at seven in the morning. Pretty early, since he didn't leave until one-thirty last night." Allie was looking at her cousin with speculation, trying to gauge the effect of her words.

"What time is it now?" Thea was really confused.

"Almost noon."

"Noon!" Thea cried. She couldn't believe it.

"The doctor said you would sleep a lot from both the injuries and the sedative. Sleep is a healing thing. And you will sleep more today." Allie's tone was firm.

"I didn't hear him come in," Thea whispered, closing her eyes. She felt drained just from her short walk and the effort of eating.

"He sat by your bed for over an hour holding your hand. He had to go to the docks, but he said he would be back this afternoon. Nicholas was very worried about you last night, and I don't think he is convinced you are not badly hurt."

Thea looked at her cousin silently, refusing to take the bait Allie was offering. She knew that her cousin wanted to make her understand how much Nicholas cared for her, but Thea knew Allie was reading too much into things.

Luckily for Thea, Allie wasn't going to argue with an injured woman. When she saw Thea start to nod her head sleepily, she carefully removed the tray and set it on the table. Allie knew that she was right about Nicholas, but she had a whole week to make her point.

Thea slept most of the afternoon and didn't wake until she felt someone's presence in the quiet room. Opening her eyes sleepily, she realized that Nicholas was sitting next to her, watching her intently.

"How long have you been here?" she asked groggily.

"For about an hour. How do you feel?" His lips were tight with concern.

Thea tried to sit up, inadvertently putting pressure on her bad shoulder. She winced, unable to suppress a slight groan of pain. Nicholas moved to help her, supporting her body against his powerful arms as easily as if she were a child. He raised the pillows and then gently rested her against them.

Thea tried to smile. "I guess if I had been stepped on by an elephant, I would feel worse."

"You gave us quite a scare, Thea," Nicholas whispered tensely, and he tightened his grip on her hand.

"I gave myself quite a scare."

In a surprisingly swift movement, Nicholas swooped down and buried his face in her hand, his lips softly kissing the bruise on her wrist. When he raised his head, his dark eyes were full of self-reproach. "God, Thea, if anything worse had happened to you, I would never have forgiven myself."

Thea was surprised and touched that he cared so much for her well-being. She tried to smile reassuringly. "I guess it's the luck of the Irish. I'm one-quarter Irish, you know."

"But you drive like a Greek," Nicholas muttered, straightening up. "And whatever made you stay so long at the site?"

"I got so interested in everything, and then it was so peaceful on the beach. I lost track of time, and forgot how bad the road was." Even in her groggy state, Thea felt sheepish. She didn't want to tell Nicholas that she had been sitting on the beach for an hour agonizing over the land sale.

"Allie told me you tried to get up this morning." Thea looked at Nicholas, and saw the anger on his face. She decided to change the subject.

"Are you upset about the car?" she asked contritely.

"Of course not! But I'm angry at you for being so foolish. You are to stay in bed! Do you understand?" When Nicholas gave an order he was used to being obeyed, and Thea had no doubt that he meant what he said. She peeked up at him, and saw the lines of fatigue etched on his face. Allie had said that he had been there at seven. She felt both guilty and touched at the depth of his concern for her.

"Nicholas, you have to rest, too," she whispered.

"I can take care of myself," Nicholas said dryly. "It's you who seems to have the problem."

Just then the door opened, and Allie came in with another tray. Thea decided that her cousin had missed her calling in life. She should have been a nurse. The tray contained a bowl of chicken soup, and the aroma floated through the room.

"Did you tell her to stay in bed?" Allie asked Nicholas, the assumption clear that he was the boss.

"Yes. And she will stay in bed even if I have to tie her to it." Nicholas took the tray from Allie and set it down in front of Thea.

"I'm really not very hungry," Thea murmured, glaring at Allie's retreating back.

Nicholas carefully folded a white napkin under her chin and ignored her words. "You have to eat, sweetheart. At least a little of this delicious soup."

"You and Allie should open a clinic," Thea muttered as he held up a teaspoon of the steaming broth. He put the spoon in her mouth and ladled up a bit more. Thea knew it was hopeless to argue with him, so she swallowed spoonful after spoonful, and she did have to admit that it was good. Whenever she faltered, Nicholas urged her on.

"The doctor said that the first day is the worst. By tomorrow you'll be gulping down ham and eggs." Carefully he wiped her chin where a drop of soup had landed, then removed the tray.

"Thank you, Nicholas," Thea said softly, moved by his careful attentiveness. He could be so firm, and then suddenly so gentle. She wanted to think about that, but she felt drowsy again. They talked for a few minutes, then Nicholas settled her back down on the bed. As she drifted off to sleep, she felt Nicholas' strong hand holding tightly onto hers.

The doctor was right. The next day she did feel much better, and, the following day, even more so. She knew that it was a losing battle to fight both Nicholas and Allie, so she resigned herself to staying in bed. In fact, it wasn't so bad. Nicholas came at least once a day, and every evening. Allie insisted that he dine at the house, so he ate with Thea every night, threatening and cajoling her when her appetite lagged. And by the third day she had no problem reading, so she tackled with real delight the novel Nicholas had brought her.

By Thursday she was allowed to go outside, and she decided to spend the entire day on the patio. In the back of her mind hovered the dark thought that John Prolisavis would be making his decision in only a few days, but she ruthlessly pushed it aside, wanting only to enjoy the sun and the fresh air. She was still on the patio when Nicholas found her that afternoon.

"You're looking much better with a little color in your cheeks," he said, kissing her on the lips.

"Oh, Nicholas, it's so lovely out here. I could sit and watch the sea for hours." Thea looked up at him happily. She was delighted to see him.

"I know what you mean." Nicholas pulled up a chair, but Thea sensed that he was a little restless.

"Would you like some coffee?" Thea reached out to

pick up the little silver bell Allie had given her to summon the maid.

"Don't have enough time, I'm afraid." His black eyes were twinkling, and Thea thought he looked like the cat who swallowed the canary. "I have to fly to Athens at five. I'm on my way to the airport."

Thea was surprised at the disappointment she felt. "How long will you be gone?"

"Until Saturday. I have some business to do on the mainland. I wouldn't leave, but you seem so much better . . ." He trailed off, suddenly looking worried.

"Of course. Don't let me stop you!" Thea thought that it was ridiculous for her to be upset just because Nicholas would be gone for less than two days.

"Is there anything you need in Athens? I'd be glad to get it for you."

"No, nothing. You have me pretty well supplied with English books." Thea grinned at him, suddenly curious as to his business. "Why are you going to Athens?"

He smiled back. "Curiosity killed the cat, Thea." Again that pleased, excited look. She wondered if it had anything to do with the land sale, and then decided that that was unfair of her. Surely he wouldn't come to gloat if he had won. Would he?

Nicholas rose from his chair, then knelt in front of her. Leaning over carefully so as to not hurt her arm, he pulled her close. "I'll certainly be happy when I can kiss you like you deserve, ma'am."

"And how's that?" Thea asked teasingly, putting her arms around his neck. She loved it when he held her close, and she also was chafing under the limitations of her accident. Thea wanted to taste one of Nicholas' strong, hard kisses just as much as he wanted to give one to her.

"You know very well," he said huskily. God, she looked so tempting, sitting there in her blue robe, her copper hair falling around her shoulders.

The patio was enclosed on two sides by the house, and the garden on the third side created a feeling of complete privacy. Nicholas glanced around, realizing that they were quite alone; then he smiled wickedly. "This is a perfect situation for a pirate. Total privacy, and a heroine who can only hobble around on one leg. I don't think I should let this opportunity pass."

"Nicholas, be good," Thea laughed, a delicious thrill of anticipation tantalizing her senses. He was pressing her into his chest, and she felt her nipples push against the material of her soft robe, eager for contact with his hard, masculine body.

"Never!" He pulled her closer and covered her lips with his. The impact of their joining sent little fires down Thea's spine, and she couldn't resist running her hand through his dark hair. "You feel so warm," he marveled, smelling the intoxicating combination of soap and sun on her skin.

"I think your kisses are giving me a fever," Thea murmured.

"A fever can be good for you," Nicholas said easily, his tongue flicking the hollow of her throat. "It helps in the healing process."

Thea's hand moved under his shirt, and she rubbed the soft hair on his chest, delighting in the sensual, silky sensation. She could feel his heart beating rapidly beneath her palm, and he held her even more tightly.

"I think I'm the one who's getting the fever," he whispered.

Thea shook her head and a smile played on her lips. "I think it could be contagious. Should we call the doctor?"

"Forget him. I think I know the cure." His eyes wandered to the soft curve of her breasts beneath the robe, and he ached to slip his hand through the enticing opening of the material. He was just about ready to act on this impulse when the maid opened the door to the patio.

Thea started guiltily, and Nicholas moved back, his annoyance at the interruption apparent. The poor girl took one look at his thunderous face and quickly retreated.

"Nicholas, I think you scared her half to death," Thea laughed.

"Serves her right," Nicholas grumbled. Then he straightened up. "Well, it's probably for the best. If I had really started kissing you, I might have missed my plane."

"Would that have been so bad?" Thea met his eyes.

"This time, yes." He offered no more in the way of explanation.

Nicholas left a few moments later, and Thea felt a distinct sense of loss. She knew that she was being silly, but she couldn't subdue the loneliness that enveloped her. She didn't like knowing that Nicholas was gone from the island.

She was still brooding in the garden when Allie came home. Her cousin was quick to notice Thea's bad mood, and she talked idly of other things, hoping that Thea would tell her what was wrong. At last, exasperated, she could contain herself no longer.

"Did you and Nicholas have a quarrel?" she asked in her usual straightforward manner.

Thea looked at her evasively. "No," she mumbled under her breath. "He had to go to the mainland on business, and he won't be back until Saturday."

Allie looked pleased. It would do Thea good to realize how much she missed Nicholas. Allie was convinced that her cousin was blind to Nicholas' real feelings, and quite possibly to the strength of her own for the handsome American. Thea knew that she loved Nicholas, but did she realize that she would probably be miserable living without him? Allie doubted it.

"You know he is crazy in love with you," she ventured with determination.

"Allie, don't start," Thea begged. "He was quite thrilled to be going to Athens. It was probably getting boring for him to be playing nursemaid to me."

So that was it, Allie thought to herself. A jealous pique because he had upped and left. Very good. "He'll be back soon," she declared with satisfaction.

"Whenever he decides to return, he will," Thea said coldly. She sat silently looking out to sea, and finally Allie gave up and went inside to help the maid with dinner.

Thea barely noticed her retreating figure. She *was* annoyed that Nicholas had left in such obviously high spirits, and she was angry at herself for feeling that way. It was childish and petty, and she didn't like those qualities in anyone, especially in herself.

There was another reason she was unhappy, too, and it concerned the reason for Nicholas' trip. What would put him in such high spirits if not good news about the land sale? Had John Prolisavis already notified him that his bid was accepted? If that was the case, he could have at least told her!

Irritably she got up and paced back and forth. Her knee was much better, and she only felt a slight twinge when she walked. Actually, right now she felt nothing. All of her attention was focused on examining the reason for Nicholas' trip to the mainland, and she became more and more convinced that he had the deal sewn up. After coming to that conclusion, she began to get angry, but not at Nicholas' success. It was the fact that he hadn't told her!

Thea's mood didn't improve as the afternoon slipped into evening. At dinner she was unusually quiet. Dimitri raised his eyebrows questioningly to his wife, but Allie just shook her head. Pleading a headache, Thea went to bed early, but sleep eluded her. She tossed and turned most of the night, torn between anger and hurt at Nicholas' cavalier attitude.

The next morning she was still fuming over the events of yesterday, and everyone in the house stayed clear of her. After breakfast she walked down to the beach and spent the morning staring out to sea, trying to calm her troubled mind. Besides being angry and hurt, she also realized that she still missed Nicholas, and that discovery added to her confusion.

How could she be so angry at him, and still be so eager to see him? she wondered. She didn't know. In fact, missing Nicholas added fuel to the fire of her anger. She felt that it was quite unfair that she should be missing the one person who made her so upset.

She was still on the beach when she heard Allie calling her name, and she glanced up, surprised to see her cousin signaling to her. Allie wanted her to return to the house. Slowly, taking care with her bad knee, she headed up the sloping hill to the patio.

To her amazement, she found John Prolisavis sitting in a wicker chair, sipping coffee with Allie. Her already low spirits plummeted even further. Well, I was right, she told herself. I knew the land deal was settled. Renewed anger at Nicholas and a sense of betrayal flooded her emotions, and she had to force herself to be cordial to Mr. Prolisavis.

"So glad to see you." John beamed at her. "Are you better?"

"Yes, thank you," Thea answered, sitting down next to him. She was trying to resign herself to the bad news.

That's why she didn't believe her ears at first. Thea was sure she hadn't heard correctly, and she turned to Mr. Prolisavis with a puzzled frown.

"So I am very pleased to inform you that you have the land. I was hoping things would work out this way, and they have. I am not a greedy man, and I searched my conscience. The money you have offered is more than adequate, and it is only right that the house should stay in your family. I'm afraid your grandmother's ghost would haunt me if I chose another path." John was thrilled to be delivering such good news, and was a little surprised at the American woman's blank expression.

Actually, Thea was in shock. This was the last thing she was prepared to hear, and she couldn't believe it. To say she felt dumbfounded was putting it mildly. Then her mind began to race. Why was Nicholas on the mainland? He probably didn't know anything about this. Or did he?

"Does Mr. Palmer know?" she asked, clearing her

throat. Her calm expression was belied by her tense grip on the chair.

Mr. Prolisavis looked guilty. "No. I haven't told him yet. I wasn't able to find him."

"He's on the mainland," Thea answered, and Mr. Prolisavis nodded, looking relieved that his bad news would be delayed.

"Isn't this wonderful?" Allie urged, although privately she had her doubts. A man's business was very important to him.

"Wonderful," Thea said awkwardly, trying to look happy. She would own the property; her dream would be fulfilled. She smiled a little crookedly at Mr. Prolisavis, who was glad the young woman finally registered some kind of pleasure at his decision. He decided that it must be the accident that was making her so quiet. Perhaps he should let her digest the news in private?

He stood and handed his cup to Allie. "We can meet with my lawyer on Monday, if that is satisfactory?" He looked inquiringly at Thea, who again seemed to have lapsed into a brooding silence. Perhaps it was the head injury, he thought to himself. The bruise on her head looked bad.

He quickly took his leave, and Allie escorted him to the door. When she returned, Thea was not on the patio. Allie looked around and spotted her cousin on the beach, pacing slowly back and forth.

Allie shook her head. What complications in this life!

Chapter Ten

Thea's thoughts echoed Allie's, except more strongly. She felt like crying, but she forced back the tears and tried to think things out as she paced on the sand. For years she had looked forward to this moment, to the day she would own her grandmother's house. It had been her cherished goal from the time she was a little girl. She used to think about it in quiet moments and make her plans.

And now she had it. It was just within her grasp. And . . . she was miserable. Overcome with dejection, Thea walked along the empty beach, lost in her thoughts. The land was hers. Yet, it was a hollow victory, for it came at Nicholas' expense.

Nicholas! How would he feel when he heard the news? This would be a major setback for him as far as his business went. The land was vital to the commercial success of his venture. She thought about his reaction and knew that he would be upset. Yet he would also be happy for her. There was an essential element of fair play in Nicholas. He wouldn't begrudge her the victory, even at the cost to himself.

But what a cost. Her troubled mind couldn't escape the truth, and instead of wanting to celebrate she felt lost and confused. True, there had been one brief moment of elation when John Prolisavis' words had sunk in. But the elation had passed in an instant, leaving a feeling of frustration. The gods who wove their fates had certainly screwed up on this one.

Thea kicked a pile of sand, and then winced as pain tore through her injured knee. She cursed her immobility, then sighed at her stupid behavior. She really could walk quite well when she didn't do silly things like physically attack intangible problems.

Nursing her injured knee, Thea sat down on a small rock and gazed out to sea. Melinas had been here for thousands of years. It had seen the rise and fall of ancient civilizations, withstood the invaders from the Middle East, and survived the occupation of the Turks, and, much later, the Germans during World War II. Through all the centuries it had endured, resting tranquilly in the heart of the Ionian Sea, beautiful and peaceful.

Her ancestors had been born on this lovely island, but they were forced to leave it, and resettle in America. And for them, their new home had been as good as the old. But they had kept a part of Melinas in their hearts, a treasured memory they would always hold dear. And it was part of Thea. Melinas was in her blood. Now that she had seen it, she knew that she would always need to come back, to renew her bonds with this magic place.

But did she really have to own a piece of land here? Wasn't the spirit of Melinas already hers—something vital that could never be destroyed? Carefully she considered every aspect of the situation.

Now that she thought about it, it didn't seem very important where she stayed when she came to Melinas. Her grandmother's property was only one very tiny portion of this island. But to Nicholas it was vital. He really needed the property by the sea.

Thea let her thoughts drift over the last week, and she recalled the festival of Diana. The sacrifices of the goddess and of St. Constantina were part of her heritage, too, and they should have taught her something. This island had survived because those women had sacrificed things they loved to help others. Could she really turn her back on their teachings and still believe she was a part of Melinas?

The answer was clear. She couldn't take the land. It simply meant too much to Nicholas. He needed his work, and he had the right to do it as well as he could. She loved him, and she wanted him to have what could have been hers. She saw no other answer to the dilemma they faced.

Thea looked out on the shimmering water, and tears filled her eyes. Yes, she really did love him. He didn't love her, but that didn't make any difference. Nicholas deserved the best she could give him. She had a life in Manhattan, a successful career. New York was where she belonged. Thea knew in her heart that if Nicholas asked, she would move heaven and earth to stay here. But he hadn't asked, and that was that.

Thea had always been one to face life's problems squarely. Now she reviewed her options, and then made her decisions. By the time she left the beach it was late afternoon, and she had made all her plans with careful deliberation. Thea wasn't happy at the turn of events, but she was satisfied that she was doing the right thing. Unfortunately, that wasn't a very comforting feeling.

If Thea was satisfied, Allie was not. "This is craziness," Allie told her bluntly, shocked that Thea would even conceive of such a plan.

"He deserves the land," Thea said quietly, taking her cousin's hand in hers. They were sitting together on the patio. The light was beginning to fade, but the sound of the waves hitting the beach reached them clearly.

"That I agree with. It is the other part I think is foolish beyond words. To sneak away to New York

and not let him know is the craziest of all things."
Allie's grasp of English failed her in her outraged
state, and she spoke a few Greek words which left no
doubt as to what she thought of her cousin's state of
mind.

"Allie, please try to understand. It will be less
painful for me this way. And for Nicholas. If I stay
around after he knows what I've done, he may feel as
though he has to persuade me to change my mind. He
may even refuse the land. He wants it, but he has a lot
of pride." And so do I, Thea thought silently. She
couldn't bear to have Nicholas feel obligated to her in
any way.

Allie ignored her cousin's words and waved her
hands in Mediterranean frustration. "But you don't
even give him a chance to say he doesn't want you. Or
does want you. You try to read his mind. It isn't fair,
Thea. The man's crazy in love with you!"

Could Allie be right? Thea considered her cousin's
words for a moment, then rejected the idea. If
Nicholas wanted her, he would have said something
before this. He'd had more than ample opportunity.

Thea shook her head sadly. "No, Allie, Nicholas
has never said he loved me. If he did, he would have
told me."

As she watched Thea's face, Allie felt the taste of
defeat. What a hardhead her cousin was! So blind to
Nicholas' love. Were all Americans so silly? Then
inspiration hit her, and she smiled hopefully. "Look
how upset he was when you were hurt. The man was
sick! All because of you."

Thea shook her head. "It was just normal concern,
Allie. He cares about me, I agree. But he isn't
thinking about a permanent relationship."

"Like marriage?" Allie wanted to understand what
Thea was really looking for in life.

Thea sat quietly for another moment, then nodded.
"Right. Like marriage."

Allie sighed, wondering just how much advice she
could morally give. Her upbringing had been strict,

but times had changed. Perhaps Thea should try to live for the moment, and marriage and children would come later. She had no doubt that Nicholas loved her cousin, even if Thea was too stupid to realize it.

Thea took advantage of Allie's silence to rise. She had spent the last hour trying to explain the wisdom of her actions, but she doubted if she could convince Allie. Now was the time to break off the conversation.

"When will you be leaving?" Allie asked, genuinely sorry to see her exasperating cousin depart.

"On Sunday. I have a reservation on the seven o'clock flight out of Melinas. And on an afternoon flight from Athens to New York." Thea had made the reservations that afternoon.

"And when will you leave from here?"

"Tomorrow morning. I have a lot to do back in town if my plan is going to work. So if you could, I'd like an early ride back to town."

Allie rose, admitting that she had lost the battle. She knew that it was useless to argue any longer, and she wondered again at her cousin's foolishness.

Dimitri drove Thea back to town the next morning. She had truly been sorry to say good-bye to Allie, who stood in the driveway with tears rolling down her plump cheeks as the pickup truck started off toward the village. Thea asked Dimitri to stop at John Prolisavis' house on the way back.

The old man was dumbfounded when Thea told him about her decision, and he wondered again if the young woman's head injury had been more severe than anyone realized. But he was also relieved. By offering the land to Thea, he had accepted a large financial loss. Now, in good conscience, he could accept Mr. Palmer's offer. He had done his duty, and the gods had provided.

"But be sure *not* to tell Mr. Palmer anything until he comes to you," Thea cautioned him a second time. She didn't want an impetuous Mr. Prolisavis to tip off Nicholas about her plans.

"Of course, of course. I understand." He didn't,

but he certainly wasn't going to argue with this crazy American.

The rest of the morning passed quickly for Thea. She knew that the local plane from Athens didn't arrive until four o'clock on Saturday, but she wanted to complete all her plans before Nicholas returned. The hotel staff was delighted to see her back, and everyone asked about her health. After politely answering their questions, Thea went up to her room and packed, carefully leaving out an outfit for the evening and a traveling suit for the trip home. She would have to leave quickly and quietly the next morning if she was to get away before Nicholas woke up.

A lump rose in her throat at the idea. It seemed incredible that tomorrow she would be gone, and Nicholas would still be here in Melinas. The idea was so upsetting she couldn't bear thinking about it. Instead, she forced herself to go over her list of things to do.

There were still some important tasks she hadn't completed. She quickly decided which one to tackle first, then went down to the lobby and waited for a private moment with the hotel manager. Trying not to feel foolish, she explained that she wanted to settle her bill and arrange for a taxi to pick her up the next morning at six. And she would prefer that no one know she was leaving.

The manager was polite and helpful, but inside he was dying of curiosity. The relationship between Thea and Nicholas had escaped no one's notice, and he was amazed that Miss Hunt would not want Mr. Palmer to know of her departure. Perhaps they had quarreled? The manager was too well-bred to ask, but maybe someone else knew the real circumstances. After Thea left his office, he hurried off to ask a few questions, only to find that his staff was as mystified as he was.

This included the waiter who had just taken her order for dinner. Yes, he told the manager after Thea had gone, the young lady said that she and Mr.

Palmer would be dining in the courtyard that evening and she had selected a special meal and paid for everything in advance. It certainly was odd, and the waiter decided to tell his night counterpart to listen closely to the conversation between Thea and Nicholas.

Thea was blind to their stares and whispers. She was forcing herself to keep moving, to go through with her plans. If she stopped and faltered, she might just decide to give in to Allie's advice and tell Nicholas everything. And that would be crazy.

Nervously she glanced at her list and saw that there were only three more things to do. She sat down at a table in the lobby and composed a note to Nicholas, carefully choosing her words. After three attempts, she was satisifed.

Dear Nicholas,

I have returned to the hotel, and want to celebrate your return to Melinas. I've arranged a special little supper in the courtyard—my treat! See you at seven.

Diana

She thought for a moment, then added a postscript.

I plan on taking a little nap before dinner, so I'll be fresh for tonight. See—I *am* following the doctor's orders.

That was just right, she thought. Nicholas would think she was resting, and wouldn't disturb her. She gave the note to the desk clerk and went on to the next item on her list.

She left the hotel and headed for the plaza. Because of her knee, she was forced to walk slowly, and it took her a while to reach her destination. It also forced her to look around and remember the happy hours that she and Nicholas had spent in the little square. Never again would they sip wine at a little table and watch the strolling crowds. The realization made her want to weep.

She finally came to the stall of the flower vendor, and memories of the night Nicholas had bought her the golden rose flooded over her. That night the legend of Diana had only been a romantic tale. Today Diana's sacrifice was Thea's reality. Very carefully, she selected the loveliest bloom.

Thea had a special reason for not wanting to see Nicholas before supper. She had orchestrated this last evening with special care, and she wanted to create just the right effect. Tonight she would be giving him a memory that would have to last. Back in the cool darkness of her hotel room, she rested on the bed and went over her plans, trying not to think that tomorrow at this time she would be somewhere over the Atlantic.

Forget tomorrow, she told herself sternly. Think about the special hours to come.

Yesterday on the quiet beach she had made the most important decision of her life. Tonight she would become Nicholas' lover. Besides the land, she wanted to give him the gift of herself. The last, most precious parting gift. She had thought about it carefully, and decided that it was what she really wanted to do.

Thea knew with absolute certainty that she would never love anyone more than she loved Nicholas, and to leave without taking the sweet memory of their union would be impossible for her to bear. She knew she had changed. Once premarital sex had seemed completely wrong to her, but now she was wiser. It was *love* that made lovemaking sacred, not marriage vows. And she loved Nicholas totally.

Tomorrow she would be gone, and Nicholas would own the land. He would settle into his new life. For him she was a tender interlude. For her, the time with Nicholas would be a memory she would always cherish.

It was time to get ready. She had hoped to nap, but sleep eluded her. She didn't really mind; she wanted to savor every moment she had left on Melinas.

Thea prepared for the evening with painstaking care. She soaked in the tub for a half hour, letting the silky bath oil soften her skin. Then she washed with scented soap, and shampooed her hair.

Stepping from the tub, Thea wrapped her hair in a Turkish towel and grimaced at her reflection in the mirror. The bruise on her forehead was still pretty ugly. There was little she could do but apply some makeup. At least the swelling had gone down and the color had improved somewhat. She applied a light foundation carefully to her face, and the discoloration was lessened. Then she put on eyeshadow, a touch of mascara, and just the lightest amount of blush. After her makeup was done, Thea did her nails, carefully applying a pale pink polish to each finger.

She glanced at the clock, and was reassured that she had plenty of time. Now for her hair. She blow-dryed it, then brushed the copper locks until they shimmered like melted gold. She arranged her hair so part of it fell over her forehead, helping to disguise the disfiguring bruise. When she was satisfied she turned to her closet, and looked at the outfit she had selected for the evening.

The turquoise halter dress was the exact shade of her eyes, with thin spaghetti straps that wouldn't irritate her still-sensitive shoulder. It was very warm today, and the dress would be nice and cool. She put on a pair of panties and then slipped on a pair of high-heeled sandals. Her knee protested slightly, but Thea ignored the pain. She would be sitting most of the evening, and she didn't want to ruin the effect of the dress with the wrong shoes.

Now for the rose. Thea plucked it from the little bud vase and wiped the water from the stem. Where would be the best place to wear it? She looked at the dress doubtfully, then inspiration hit her. After she trimmed the stem, Thea carefully pulled back the hair on the uninjured side of her face, and clipped it with a barrette. She placed the rose in her hair, securing the stem behind her ear. The golden petals blended perfectly with her own copper locks, and the effect was exactly what she had desired.

Pleased with her appearance, Thea smiled, anticipating Nicholas' reaction. Then her face clouded. She had almost forgotten that she had one last thing to do. The most important item on her list. She sat down at the little table next to the bed and took out some note paper. Then, concentrating carefully because she wanted to choose just the right words, Thea began to compose her last letter to Nicholas.

His expression told her immediately that he found her beautiful. When she walked into the courtyard Nicholas was already there, waiting impatiently, his eyes riveted on the door. When he saw Thea he jumped up from the table. Oblivious to everyone else around, he strode toward her and pulled her into his powerful arms, giving her a warm kiss of welcome.

"It seems like I've been waiting for hours," he said eagerly, his gaze moving over her body with delight. "I thought seven o'clock would never come."

He was dressed in a pair of fawn-colored slacks and a navy blue shirt open at the collar, and he looked very handsome. Thea felt a lump grow in her throat as she remembered that this would be the last time they would be dining together, but she ruthlessly suppressed it. She refused to spoil the night with thoughts of tomorrow!

Instead, she willed herself to be happy. "What time did you return?" she asked as Nicholas guided her to their table.

"I was back at the hotel around four-thirty, and was ready to rush to Allie's house when I found your note." They sat down, drawing their chairs close to one another, and Nicholas took Thea's hand in his. "Are you going to tell me what this little celebration is all about?"

Thea had planned her response to this question carefully. "It's a little thank-you party for all you did for me when I was injured." She kept her voice light. "I thought you would appreciate a quiet, romantic dinner after all the nights you spent eating with a plate on your lap."

"I can imagine better circumstances with you in bed," Nicholas said dryly, raising his eyebrows. "But I certainly never minded. The only thing I didn't like were the hours I had to spend away from you." Thea flushed at his words, imagining all too well the circumstances he was referring to, and the thought of what she had planned for later tonight made her cheeks turn crimson.

Nicholas read her mind, though he had no idea that his dreams were going to turn to reality. In a soft silky tone calculated to arouse, he continued. "You and I are thinking of the same thing, aren't we, Thea? The last week has been a tremendous tease. Not intentionally, but a tease nonetheless."

"I didn't think I looked that good to you, all laid up." Thea wanted to break the spell he was weaving around her. It was too soon; she had the entire night to spend with Nicholas.

"I wasn't looking at your bruises," he commented softly. "Don't you think your body was visible under the sheer nightgown Allie gave you? Every time I came close to you . . ." He broke off abruptly, the memory just a little too tantalizing for a man sitting in the middle of a hotel courtyard.

Thea had wondered about the nightgown. It had been made of soft cream-colored silk which molded to the contours of her body. When she had asked Allie if perhaps it was too fine, her cousin had evasively answered that it was all she had. Allie at work again. Thea changed her opinion of the career that Allie should take up. Instead of nursing, she should run for local matchmaker.

Just then the waiter brought a delicious plate of appetizers, and Thea carefully selected a piece of marinated shrimp. "I ordered the entire dinner," she told Nicholas. "I hope you don't mind."

"Not at all. At times I love to be pampered." His

caressing tone suggested a great deal more than his actual words, and for one moment a vivid picture of the night to come flashed in Thea's mind. She turned scarlet, and Nicholas looked at her curiously, surprised at her reaction to his teasing.

Thea groped for something to say. "Was your trip to Athens successful?" She really was curious about the business which had caused him to leave so abruptly.

Nicholas' eyes sparkled, and Thea saw the same satisfied look she had noticed when he told her about the trip. "Yes, I think it was."

She couldn't stop herself from asking. "Why did you go?"

He looked at her speculatively for a moment before answering, and then his tone was light and teasing. "I'll tell you all about it tomorrow. I have my surprises, too."

Thea tried to keep her face politely curious. But inside, her heart was crying. *There will be no tomorrow, Nicholas. Not for us. We want different things in life.*

Even though she tried to hide it, Nicholas was quick to sense the change in her mood. "Thea, what is it?" he asked with concern. "Don't you feel well?"

"I'm just a little tired, that's all."

Nicholas looked doubtful for a moment, but then continued enthusiastically. "I thought we could go out on the boat, if you feel well enough. Then have a quiet picnic on the beach."

Thea looked down at her plate, trying to get control of herself. She had to carry this off!

"Do you think it would be too much for you?" Nicholas asked, taking her hand in his. "We could go to the beach by car." He gently pushed back the lock of copper hair covering her forehead. "That bruise still looks pretty bad."

She didn't want to lie to him outright. "No, the bruise looks worse than it is. Really." She tapped her fingers nervously on the table.

She was saved by the sudden appearance of the

waiter, who wheeled in their dinner on a cart. Thea had ordered the house specialty, a rack of lamb with rice pilaf. Cherry tomatoes, Greek cheese, and black olives colorfully garnished the dishes. She forced herself to be gay, and Nicholas, flattered that she had gone to so much trouble for him, dropped the subject of tomorrow.

The meal went very well, although Thea ate little. Nicholas noticed her apparent lack of appetite, and also that she drank an extra glass of wine. He asked again whether she was feeling well.

"No, I feel fine," she said, smiling a trifle giddily. The wine was stronger than she had thought. "I just haven't had too great an appetite since the accident." She didn't mention that it was really nerves which kept her appetite at bay.

The sun was setting and a waiter was busy lighting the red candles at each table, creating a soft, romantic light over the courtyard. Thea's eyes turned toward the marble statue of Diana, and she almost thought she saw a sad expression flicker over the face of the goddess.

"You're far more beautiful than she is," whispered Nicholas, following her look.

"Don't say that," Thea said. But she was still pleased at his words. "You don't want to make the gods jealous. Especially the Greek gods. They might turn me into a spider out of spite."

"I wouldn't let them." Nicholas had taken her hand in his, and his fingers were tracing a tantalizing pattern on the palm of her hand.

Thea sat back, pleasantly relaxed on one level, yet tense on another, deeper one. The night was going quickly. They had already finished their meal, and were now enjoying coffee and liqueurs. Soon they would go upstairs, and she wondered if she could play out this part without making Nicholas suspicious. He knew her so well. It wouldn't be like her to set aside her convictions.

Finally the moment couldn't be delayed any longer. It was close to ten o'clock. Trying to look calm but feeling like she was a bundle of nerves, Thea smiled at Nicholas. "Are you ready for the rest of your surprise?"

He looked up at her, startled. "There's more?"

"Oh, yes. But it's not down here." Thea looked into his eyes, and read the question there. She felt herself flush. "Are you ready to go?"

"The check?"

"It's all taken care of," Thea answered quickly. "I told you this was my treat."

"Ah, women's lib," Nicholas laughed. "All right. Just this one time."

Thea's heart lurched in her chest at his words. This one last time, she thought bleakly.

Nicholas took her arm, and tenderly helped her from the table. "So where is the rest of my surprise?"

"You'll see."

They walked toward the balcony steps, Nicholas following Thea with a mystified expression on his face. It seemed like they were heading for his room. They *were* heading for his room!

Thea looked ahead, pleased that the bellboy had followed her instructions. A little bar cart stood next to Nicholas' door, and two glasses and an ice bucket with champagne were visible.

"Aha," Nicholas said with satisfaction. "A quiet little nightcap." He looked delighted, and Thea smiled.

Then she jumped at his next words. "Would you like me to get two chairs so we can sit and look at the garden below?"

My God, he was making this difficult. She could have kissed him and hit him at the same time. How did women ever successfully seduce men? No wonder it was usually the other way around!

"No, let's have it inside."

Nicholas shot her a glance, and Thea held her breath. "Are you sure?" he asked quietly. "You're tempting fate."

"I'm sure." She could barely hear her own voice.

As Nicholas wheeled the little bar cart in, Thea

forced herself to keep calm by looking around his room. It was larger than hers, and better furnished. He lit a small lamp, and the light was warm and inviting. The room contained a chair and a large double bed covered with a soft, golden quilt.

"Why don't you sit down?" he said, pointing to the bed. "I'll open the champagne."

Thea looked at the bed as if it were on fire, and Nicholas laughed. "Come on, sweetheart, I'll be good. You'll be more comfortable there. You can put your knee up. I saw you wince as we climbed the stairs." He plumped up the pillows, and Thea kicked off her sandals and sat down on the coverlet, stretching her legs out in front of her.

He's going to be good, she thought, and I'm trying to tempt him! Her heart fluttered nervously. She glanced at Nicholas, who was still totally innocent about her intentions. He was expertly opening the champagne bottle, and, in spite of herself, she couldn't suppress a giggle when the cork flew across the room.

He laughed along with her, and brought two glasses filled with the bubbly wine over to the bed. "Move over, darling. I'm tired, too." He sat down next to her and stretched out his long legs.

"Now what should we toast?" he asked. "I have a good one, but it will have to wait until tomorrow."

Tomorrow again! Did he have to keep talking about tomorrow?

"How about to us?" Thea ventured.

Nicholas kissed her lightly on the forehead. "Yes, to us."

They clinked glasses, and Thea tasted the slightly dry champagne. Because she was nervous, she drank it quickly, and then felt even more dizzy.

"Easy, Thea. You aren't much of a drinker. This stuff will go to your head."

"I think it already has." Thea rested her head against Nicholas' shoulder, and delighted in the familiar warmth of his body.

Abruptly he finished off his glass of champagne and

set it on the table. Then he turned toward her and took her in his arms, careful not to disturb her bad shoulder. He buried his face in her hair. Then his lips trailed down to hers, and she clung to him eagerly as he teased her mouth with his hot tongue.

"I missed you while I was gone," he murmured in her ear. His voice was husky.

"And I missed you," Thea answered, raising her arms around his neck. The movement pushed her breasts upward, giving Nicholas a teasing glimpse of their round whiteness. He groaned, and his lips moved downward, tasting the softness of her skin just above the neckline of her dress. His hand went out and surrounded one full, high mound, and Thea could feel his body tense with excitement.

Thea threw back her head, straining for his touch, and shifted her weight. They were now lying side by side, facing each other, and the dizziness overcoming her wasn't from the champagne. She felt Nicholas' hand move against her thigh, and her skin tingled where his fingers touched naked skin. His hand slipped under her dress.

"My god, Thea, how I want you!" he said hoarsely, his body now taut with desire. "You're too much of a temptation."

"I want to tempt you, Nicholas," she whispered, drawing her mouth to his. She felt his body stiffen with surprise, and then he pulled her to him with unrestrained passion. She gasped, and for one moment she thought that she would drown in the pleasure of his savage embrace.

But only for one wild moment. With a groan of frustration, he let go of her abruptly and pushed himself upright.

"Nicholas, what's wrong?" Thea's eyes filled with tears.

"Thea, not tonight. Not yet, sweetheart." Nicholas cupped her face in his hand and smiled down at her. "Not tonight. Believe me, Thea, I want to make love to you. But I won't."

There was nothing Thea could say. She wouldn't

force herself on him. He really didn't love her at all. He knew her convictions, and since he wasn't going to marry her, he wouldn't make love to her.

He turned off the light, and pulled the coverlet over them. "I'd say we should get undressed, but there *is* a limit to my willpower. Let's get some sleep."

Nicholas pulled Thea close, and although she lay rigid in his arms, she felt him slowly relax and eventually fall asleep. The minutes ticked by as hot tears rolled down her face. Even with this ultimate rejection, she still lacked the strength to leave his side. The hours they had left together were too precious.

As the night wore on, exhaustion took its toll, and Thea fell into a drowsy light sleep. But part of her mind was always conscious of the clock, and when it reached five she slipped out of bed, careful not to disturb Nicholas. He murmured a slight protest when her warm body left his side, but he quickly fell back into a deep sleep.

Forcing herself to be careful and quiet, Thea laid the note she had written on the table. It would tell Nicholas about the land she was turning over to him, and that she was returning to New York. Then she removed the golden rose from her hair and set it on the note. Tiptoeing silently, she picked up her purse and shoes and walked to the door. Thea didn't allow herself a backward glance. She couldn't bear the pain.

Chapter Eleven

For Thea the next two hours were divided between misery and nervous apprehension. She was terrified that Nicholas would get up early and discover she had left, and yet, she was half hoping he would find her note, and rush after her. It was an impossible situation. After leaving his room she made her way along the balcony, almost blinded by her own tears, and by the darkness. It was still a few minutes before sunrise.

Once in her own room, she changed quickly, pulling off the turquoise dress and throwing it into her suitcase. She had laid out her traveling suit, and now she put it on. Not long ago she had dressed in the same white linen suit and pink blouse, filled with happiness and excitement about her trip to Melinas. She had thought the trip would accomplish a lifelong dream. Instead, it had changed her life.

She looked at her watch, and saw that it was ten to six. She had ordered the taxi for six o'clock to give herself plenty of time to get to the airport. Finally satisfied that she had packed everything, Thea went into the bathroom and looked at her ravaged face.

Although there was little she could do about the bruise, she didn't want anyone to see her red, swollen eyes. Even though the sun was barely up, she put on a pair of sunglasses, and then ran a comb through her tousled hair.

Thea took one more look around the suddenly dear room, then picked up her suitcase and travel bag. Forcing herself to keep moving, she walked outside. She could see Nicholas' room across the courtyard, but there was no sign of movement. He had been exhausted last night from his trip. She hoped that he was still sleeping soundly.

By the time Thea got to the lobby the taxi was waiting. She was surprised to see Andreo, the driver who had brought her and Nicholas to the village. So many reminders!

Thankful that she had settled her bill the day before, Thea quickly walked outside. Andreo stashed her luggage in the Jeep, and smiled at her inquiringly. "Mr. Palmer. Is he ready?"

Thea thought she would cry again, but she forced her words to come out calmly. "Mr. Palmer is staying on Melinas."

For one awful moment Andreo looked as if he were going to give his opinion of that decision, then thought better of it. With gallant courtesy he helped Thea into the taxi, and leaped into the front seat.

In a few moments they were off, and once again, Thea doubted that she would make it to the airport alive. Although the plane didn't leave for an hour and the ride was only about twenty minutes long, Andreo drove as if the hounds of hell were at his heels. As they lurched around a particularly bad turn, Thea recalled that first ride, when she and Nicholas had just met. It had been his strong arm which had protected her then, and kept her from flying out of the careening Jeep. She felt terribly alone, and even the incredible beauty of the Ionian Sea at sunrise could not move her.

Her thoughts were back at the hotel with Nicholas. What would he do when he discovered the note she had left? Would he understand? He might even be relieved. He cared about her, but she was a complication in his life that he didn't need.

Dismally she recalled last night and her well-laid plans. All had come to naught. Nicholas had refused the invitation she had offered with such love. Her cheeks turned red with humiliation. What would he think of her when he read the note? When he discovered that she had planned to leave all along, would he decide that she had been seducing him for one last fling? She felt terrible at the thought. It hadn't been that way for her at all. She had just wanted to love him totally before she left.

In spite of her doubts about arriving at the airport in one piece, they were there before she knew it. It was only six-thirty, but the plane was waiting. Since she was the only passenger she had her choice of places to sit, but once settled, she kept shifting nervously in her seat, her eyes straying constantly to the road, straining to see if Nicholas had followed her.

For one moment she thought she had been discovered. A red car came hurtling down the airport drive, and Thea's heart skipped a beat. She peered from the window, trying to see, but it turned out to be another Greek taxi carrying a young German tourist. The man boarded the plane and smiled at Thea and was puzzled by the cold nod she gave in response.

Even though she kept telling herself that she didn't want Nicholas to pursue her, she felt a moment of terrible disappointment when the pilot started the engines of the small plane. This was it, then. She was leaving Melinas, and the part of her life she had shared with Nicholas was over. Perhaps someday she would return, but it wouldn't be the same. Their lives would have changed entirely.

At precisely seven o'clock the little Piper Cub took off down the runway, and then they were in the air. As the plane gained altitude, and headed out to sea, Thea twisted in her seat to better see the island of Melinas growing smaller below her. Again it reminded her of a perfect jewel set in a turquoise sea.

The sun was much brighter now, and it caught the steeple of the church in the village. It seemed to Thea like a beacon calling her back, and her throat filled with unshed tears. Nicholas was so close to that beacon. As the island grew smaller and smaller, she was glad of the sunglasses. She couldn't stop the tears in her eyes from overflowing.

The rest of the short flight was lost on Thea. She felt drained. Dismally she acknowledged how much she had been hoping that Nicholas would find her note and rush after her. But he hadn't. And there was no way he could reach her now. This was the only flight from Melinas to Athens on Sunday. Well, she had made her decision, and she had to live with it. The sooner she started making the best of things, the better.

They arrived in Athens a little before eight, and Thea forced herself to look for the Acropolis. The morning sun had touched the Parthenon so that it appeared to be pink. When she and Nicholas had shared the flight to Melinas, the temple had seemed to be made of gold. Thea thought for one moment of the golden rose. Perhaps the golden temple had been an omen.

Before she could think about it any further they were descending into Athens Airport, and she prepared for the landing. They had to circle several times, but Thea felt no sense of urgency. Her flight for New York didn't leave until two o'clock Athens time. Her problem on the ground would be trying to fill all the hours she had to wait until takeoff.

Thea smiled. At least this was a little different from the day she had arrived. Then she had been rushed for time.

At last they landed. Thea picked up her flight bag and purse and headed for the door. In a few moments she was in the busy terminal, and the noise and crowds were almost a physical shock to her senses. It was amazing how several weeks on Melinas had gotten her used to peace and quiet, and a slower pace of life. What was she going to do when she got back to Manhattan?

Well, she'd worry about it later. Right now she needed something hot to drink. She made her way to the cafeteria and got a cup of coffee and a breakfast roll. She stretched the coffee out to three cups, purposely lingering over each one. But when she was finally finished, it was only nine o'clock. She still had hours to kill.

After checking in at the flight desk, Thea decided that the next stop would be the ladies' room. She had no real interest in looking terrific, but she put on some makeup anyway. It was better to look good; it always raised one's spirits, and hers certainly needed a little lift. After repairing her face, she headed for a newsstand and spent some time making her selections. When she was done, she had bought the *New York Times*, and a novel she had been wanting to read for ages.

She found a corner of the terminal where there were still some seats, and attacked the *Times* with a vengeance. When she was done she opened up the novel, and settled in for a long read. Reading would help her get through the long wait. She noticed that the Athens airport was unusually crowded. It must be all the tourists returning to the States, she thought. It was the end of summer.

Thea tried to lose herself in her book, but all the bustle and noise made it difficult to concentrate and she kept looking up, distracted by the commotion.

At one point she was disturbed by the cries of a wailing child. She looked up again, and her glance happened to rest on a young couple with their arms around each other. The man reminded her of a young version of Nicholas. Younger and much less sophisticated. He was wearing a dark blue suit with a white carnation in his lapel. His companion was a petite brunette in a white linen suit, and she was gazing up at the man with adoration. On her shoulder was a corsage of white roses.

Newlyweds, Thea thought bleakly, studying the pair. They were obviously on their honeymoon. Totally lost in each other, they were oblivious to the surrounding crowds. As she watched them, Thea felt a sharp pain well up in her chest. They looked so happy, and they should. Their dream had become reality. Normally she would be delighted for them, but today it was more than she could stand. It brought home her own situation with painful clarity.

Suddenly the airport terminal was starting to close in on her and she couldn't sit there a single moment longer. She knew that there were benches outside, so she quickly headed for the door.

Much to her relief, it was quieter outside. She could hear traffic and the sun was hot, but it was far better than being inside. And, more importantly, she wouldn't have to watch young lovers on their honeymoon.

Dispiritedly, Thea reopened her book, and tried to find the spot where she had left off. It took her a little while, but soon she was fairly content. Unwilling to break the peace she had found, she decided to skip lunch. It would be far better to remain outside.

It was a little after one o'clock when Thea finally closed her book and looked at her watch. She had better hurry. Her flight would be boarding soon. Gathering her things together, she took one last breath of the air of Greece. But here in Athens it was smoggy and filled with car exhaust. Quite unlike the sweet air of Melinas.

Dismally she wondered if she would spend her life comparing things with what she had found on Melinas.

Once she was back inside, the crowds of people seemed even worse, and she felt suffocated. As she made her way to the boarding gate, loudspeakers were blaring in several different languages, and the noise added to the confusion of the crowds. It seemed to take forever to reach the gate, and once there Thea had to face a long boarding line. This was going to be a crowded flight, she thought miserably.

Long ago Thea had discovered that spending time in line went much faster if she studied those in line with her and tried to guess their professions. It was a way to keep amused, and now she started, selecting the person farthest up in line whom she could see. She was working on her fourth selection when she heard a commotion by the ramp nearest her.

She turned. It looked like someone had been jostled in the large crowd, and was complaining loudly. And then she looked closer, and couldn't believe her eyes.

Striding through the crowd with an anxious frown on his face was Nicholas. His eyes were scanning the area frantically, and just as she realized it was he, he spotted her. Even from a distance, she could see the relief on his face.

It took him only an instant to reach her, and before she could say a word, she was wrapped in his strong arms. "Thea, are you completely crazy?" she heard him whisper, his voice husky with emotion.

She couldn't reply. Surprise and pleasure had effectively cut off all sound in her throat, and she could only cling to him, totally overcome by his arrival.

"Come on, we're leaving." Nicholas released her, but his arms remained around her waist. He was looking down at her, the relieved expression softening the lines of strain etched on his face.

We're leaving. The words sounded so wonderful to Thea's ears. It was a magical reprieve from the trip she dreaded. But she couldn't leave. Nothing had been resolved. Nicholas had no right just to pluck her from this line and whisk her away. She looked up at him, trying to find the right words.

"Thea, did you hear me? We're going home." Nicholas' tone dared her to defy him, but there was amusement in his dark eyes.

Thea took a deep breath. "No, Nicholas. Home for me is in Manhattan. Melinas is your home."

His expression was disbelieving, and he tightened his grip on her shoulders. "Thea . . ." he began.

"No, Nicholas." She was firm. "What you want

from our relationship and what I want are two different things. I won't come back to Melinas and be your mistress. That's not what I want in life."

"Thea, do you love me?" His words were soft.

She couldn't believe that he would dare to ask her such a question when he had never said those magic words himself. She looked up at him defiantly. He wasn't going to leave her with any pride at all.

"Answer me." Now his voice was demanding, and his black eyes bored into hers.

Thea couldn't draw her eyes from his face, and, in spite of herself she answered him honestly. "Yes, Nicholas, I do love you."

"Then trust me enough to come with me."

The crowd began to push forward, and Thea tried to release herself from Nicholas' grip. "Nicholas, I have to go! Please!" Hot tears burned her eyes so that she could barely see.

"Damn it, woman, I'm not going to propose to you in the middle of an airport lobby," he roared, shaking her slightly to drive some sense into her uncomprehending brain.

Thea stopped dead in her tracks, not believing her ears. She looked at Nicholas with a dumbfounded expression on her face. "Propose?" she asked blankly.

"Propose," Nicholas repeated emphatically. "That's what I've been planning to do since I returned to Melinas. Except that you spoiled all my plans by running away."

"Oh, my God," Thea whispered, the realization making her almost speechless. Then wild elation flooded through her, and she wrapped her arms around Nicholas. Oblivious to all the staring people, they clung to each other.

Finally, after a long moment, Nicholas gently disengaged himself. "Now will you come with me? Our plane is waiting."

"Waiting?" Thea asked blankly. It suddenly dawned on her to question how Nicholas had gotten here. She had taken the only scheduled flight from Melinas.

"Yes, waiting," Nicholas said, taking her by the arm. "I had to charter a plane to come after you. If you only knew all the phone calls I had to make to find one! It took me forever to reach Mike Donell, my old friend from Springfield."

They didn't have time to say anything more as they rushed for the plane. Then Thea remembered her baggage. "Nicholas, my suitcase, all my clothes. They're on the other plane," she cried.

"Trust me. I took care of it." He hurried her forward, then suddenly remembered her bad knee. With a low curse he scooped her up in his arms and began to carry her through the busy terminal, ignoring the astounded looks of the other travelers.

First Thea laughed in surprise, then at the ridiculous picture they must be making. But she didn't care. She felt like an old-fashioned heroine being abducted by her hero.

"You were so sure, then?" she asked, nuzzling against his broad chest.

"Of what?" He was holding her as easily as a feather as they walked.

"That I would come with you."

"I couldn't bear to think you wouldn't. You had to come back."

Thea smiled happily, and they didn't speak again until they were comfortably settled in the little plane. The pilot was eager to return home, and the plane took off as soon as clearance was given.

"Now tell me everything," Thea said, holding onto Nicholas' hand as if she were afraid to let go. In fact, she *was* afraid to let go! She still half believed that this was all some sort of wonderful hallucination.

"Do you want me to start from when I first saw your note, or when I let out a curse that woke the people in the next three rooms?" Nicholas' tone was dry, but he was watching her intently.

"Nicholas, I'm sorry. I thought I was doing the

right thing." Thea was sincerely penitent. "I thought you didn't love me, and I wanted you to have the land. I was afraid if I told you, you might feel obligated to ask me to stay."

"Obligated? That's the last way I feel about you. Your cousin Allie was right. You really are foolish."

"You spoke to Allie?" Thea was dying to fit all the missing pieces of the puzzle together.

"Yes. She was the first person I called. She told me what had happened with John Prolisavis and about your flight plans. Then I called Mike. I couldn't reach him until ten o'clock, and by then I was panicking. I paged you at the airport . . ."

"I was outside," Thea told him. "I couldn't stand the crowds."

Nicholas shrugged. "I didn't know why they couldn't find you, but I ordered them to take your luggage off the plane, and send it back to Ionian Airways. Then I found Mike, and he got to Melinas at twelve-thirty. It was really close."

"Part of me was praying that you would follow me," Thea admitted quietly.

"My goodness, woman, you cause me more trouble than any other person I've met in my life." Somehow Nicholas made it sound like a compliment and an accusation all at the same time.

Thea bristled. "If you had been clearer about your intentions, we never would have had this problem." Her blue eyes flashed fire.

"I never dreamed you'd pull such a stunt," he said softly, leaning toward her. His warm lips settled on hers. Nicholas had meant it to be only a light kiss, but he couldn't resist lingering and lingering. . . . They were a good deal closer to Melinas when Thea pulled away from him.

"Nicholas, we're in the middle of the air," she protested with a smile, really not caring at all where they were.

"You were certainly eager enough last night," he teased, his lips moving to her ear.

Thea blushed. So she had been. And still was. But

not at three thousand feet. "I thought you didn't want me," she confessed.

Nicholas laughed out loud and pushed her back so he could see her face. "Not want you! I wanted you so badly that I didn't trust myself to hold off. Thank God I was exhausted from the trip."

"Then why did you say no?" Thea had to ask.

"Because I knew how you felt, and I wanted it to be the right time for you in every way."

"I had planned everything so carefully," Thea murmured in self-disgust. "If only I had been a little more honest, this never would have happened."

Nicholas smiled wryly, then slipped his arm around her shoulder. "That makes two of us. I had my proposal all planned out, and I didn't want to change it. I thought it was so romantic."

Suddenly everything dawned on Thea, and she gasped. "You mean you were going to propose on the beach?"

"Exactly. On the very spot where we had our first picnic." He looked at her warmly. "I guess I wasn't very honest, either."

"You were honest," Thea defended him. "You just left out a few pertinent details."

Again Nicholas reached over and drew Thea back into his arms and rested his cheek against her hair. She could feel his heart beating rapidly against her chest. "I love you, Thea. I've loved you since the first time I laid eyes on you. I just didn't realize how much."

"Oh, Nicholas, I love you, too," Thea said softly, tears of happiness in her eyes. He loved her. Love was all that mattered. Then another thought followed quickly, and she knew she had to tell him.

"Nicholas, if you love me, love is enough. We'll have time later to think of marriage. I was being foolish."

"Are you backing out on me, lady?" he asked, his black eyes flashing. "Cause I'll charter planes all over the world, and follow you until you say yes."

"I do say yes, Nicholas," Thea laughed, delighted

with his reaction. "But marriage is a big step, and I want you to be sure." What if he were proposing because he thought it was the only way to keep her? If he didn't want marriage, and was forced into it . . .

He looked at her lovingly, reading her mind. "Thea, I'm very sure. I have been for days. This isn't a spur of the moment thing. I had even thought about giving up the land to you. But when I knew I wanted to marry you, I knew we could share everything together."

"Really?"

Nicholas didn't answer. Instead, he released Thea, and reached into his pocket. "I almost forgot this in my hurry to catch the plane. I ordered it last week, the day after your accident. This is what I went to Athens to pick up."

Nicholas held out a tiny white box, and Thea felt her hands shake as she took it. She opened it slowly, then felt a wave of happiness come over her. It was a moment before she could speak, and then it was only in a voice choked with emotion. "Oh, Nicholas, it's incredibly beautiful."

Lying nestled in the center of the box was a diamond ring. The perfect stone had a brilliance that was breathtaking. But the part which touched Thea the most was the setting. It was made of gold, with tiny leaves interwoven around the diamond, creating a flower. As Nicholas placed it on the third finger of her left hand Thea stared at the ring in wonder. She was wearing the golden rose.

Thea poured herself another cup of coffee and strolled out to the patio. It was late afternoon. She loved this time of day, when the sun would sparkle on the water, and the cool sea breeze drifted up from the beach. Sighing with satisfaction, she sat down and glanced at her list of things to do. Redecorating the old house kept her very busy. But she had accomplished all she had planned for the day, and she deserved a few minutes of peace.

Her eyes drifted down past the olive trees to the beach. There were two yachts anchored in the water, but they only added to the beauty of the scene. Like her they were secure and peaceful in their safe harbor.

The construction of Nicholas' business was almost complete, and already the docking areas were half full. And soon she would be back at work, managing the Melinas version of The Magnificent Mermaid. Both she and Nicholas thought it would be an excellent addition to the Palmer Charter Boat Company.

It really didn't seem possible that three months had passed, and she was really living on Melinas. But when you crowded so much into twelve weeks, time did appear to pass quickly. Let's see, she mused, we've been living in Grandmother's house for almost five weeks. And we were married six weeks ago.

After that incredible day at the Athens airport, she and Nicholas had returned to Melinas to make their wedding plans. Allie had been wildly enthusiastic, but clearly disappointed when Nicholas and Thea decided to get married in the States.

"We really have to, Allie," Thea explained to her cousin. "After all, we do have to go back to settle things. And our families live in America."

Nicholas and Thea had planned a small, intimate affair, but Thea was still amazed at the amount of work that even a tiny wedding entailed. Nicholas hadn't been able to resist teasing her about all the things she worried about.

"Why don't we just elope, and move to a desert island?" he had said, nibbling on her ear.

"Nicholas, we are moving to an island. Not a desert island, to be sure, but an island, nonetheless." Thea had been both amused and irritated by his complete lack of interest in the details of the wedding.

"I couldn't care less if you got married in a barrel or in a Dior gown. The only thing I care about is marrying you. Period. And isn't that enough?"

Thea had looked up at his laughing black eyes and warm sensuous mouth, and decided that it certainly was enough. More than enough. The discussion of the wedding ended in a warm embrace going on far into the night.

That had been six weeks ago. And these past weeks on Melinas had been better than any official honeymoon Thea had ever heard about. They had decided to spend a week at the Ionian Inn, and then move right into her grandmother's house. Nicholas gave her carte blanche on the redecorating.

"It's my wedding gift to you, Thea. You gave me the land, and I'm giving it back to you."

Thea had been moved to tears by his beautiful gesture, and quickly decided that the best way to repay him was to make the old house into the best home she could create. It had been both a challenge and a joy.

And as she thought about it now, the only room that still needed work was the bathroom. Nicholas had insisted on an American shower, and it was being ordered. The rest of the bathroom was going to be done in pink and white marble, and it would be a little oasis of luxury for them both. The piece de résistance was a sunken marble tub.

Thea smiled dreamily. Nicholas had argued for the tub very persuasively, and she felt a little rush of anticipation warm her body.

"And what are you smiling about, my dear?" Nicholas' lips against her neck brought her back to reality. He had walked around the side of the house, and she hadn't heard him.

"Oh, just a little daydreaming about the sunken tub." Thea smiled up at him. Nicholas was wearing jeans and a blue denim shirt rolled up at the sleeves, and he was looking at her with an intrigued expression.

"I know that little smile," he said, taking her hand and lifting her from the wicker chair. Thea was wearing white shorts and a blue halter top. She was barefoot, and so she came just to his shoulder. "What was it about the tub that made you smile like that?"

"Hmm," Thea murmured, nestling her head

against his chest. As always, he smelled like the sun and the sea. "You'll find out."

"I want to know now!" His tanned hand cupped her chin, turning her face upward.

"You're home early," Thea teased him, changing the subject.

"You little minx, answer me."

"Not until you let me show you what I bought today," Thea said smiling. She knew Nicholas was amused at the game they were playing.

"Okay," Nicholas sighed.

Thea really did want to show him something new. Besides the interior of the house, she had been redoing the patio area and the garden. It was to the garden that she now led him. Nicholas followed her, curious to see what she had bought.

"They look like rose bushes to me," he said, puzzled.

"They are. The golden rose variety," Thea replied. "I bought them today. Six of them."

"Why six?"

"To celebrate our anniversary." Thea smiled happily. "Wasn't it a wonderful idea?"

"Wonderful," Nicholas agreed. Then he reached toward her and pulled her close. Just before his lips touched hers, he spoke. "But I can think of a better way to celebrate our anniversary."

With one fluid movement he lifted her into his arms and carried her toward the house. "Nicholas, what about dinner?" Thea laughed, delighted with the turn of events.

"We'll go out for dinner. To the taverna in the plaza. Unless Allie invites us to her house again. You know she always calls about an hour before dinner and asks us to come over. By the way, that reminds me." They had just entered the coolness of the house, and Nicholas walked over to the phone, and with one hand, carefully removed the receiver. "I don't want any interruptions."

"I don't know why we bothered to install a phone, you take it off the hook so often," Thea laughed.

With a quick stride he moved into the bedroom, and deposited Thea on the bed. She sank into the soft coverlet and watched her husband slowly unbutton his shirt. "Even though we don't have a sunken tub, yet, I do think a shower is in order," Nicholas said huskily. "Do you agree?"

"Anything you say, darling."

As Thea removed her halter top and shorts, Nicholas found that he couldn't tear his eyes away from her tanned, curving body. He stopped undressing and just watched her as she removed each garment. His eyes were like dark, burning coals.

When she was totally naked, she turned toward him, and smiled. "Well?"

With a growl he peeled off his tight jeans, and in moments they were both under the warm, pulsating spray.

Later, lying contentedly in bed, her body nestled in the crook of Nicholas' arm, Thea watched the sun set over the Ionian Sea. The view from the bedroom window was marvelous, and she loved to watch both the sunset and the dawn, while she felt the warmth of Nicholas' body next to hers.

Everything was peaceful here on Melinas, she thought dreamily. The pace of life was slow, and there was time for moments like these. And these were the moments that made life worthwhile.

"What are you thinking about?" Nicholas asked drowsily, pulling her closer.

Thea nestled in his arms and felt his heart beating against her ear. It was a marvelous, comforting sound. "Just how happy I am. And how everything has worked out so well for both of us. I don't think I could ask for anything more."

"Well, I could," Nicholas murmured, his breath hot against her cool skin. One tanned hand cupped her soft breast, and his fingers gently stroked her nipple.

"Nicholas, you're incorrigible," Thea smiled, running her fingers over the dark, curling hair on his chest.

"Are you complaining?" He boosted himself on one elbow, but his hand remained on her breast, kneading it with slow, teasing movements.

Thea looked up at him and studied his face in the darkening shadows of the room. He still reminded her of a Greek god. That was what she had thought the very first time they had met. "No, Nicholas, I'm not complaining at all. You know that."

"Yes, I did, but I wanted to hear you say it."

"Why?" she laughed as he pulled her even closer, and their bodies molded together under the soft linen sheet.

He didn't answer for a long moment. Instead, his lips traced a hot pattern of kisses along her neck, both teasing and exciting her. Then his lips moved up to hers and she heard him sigh. "Because I love you, Thea. Because I love you."

Silhouette Romance

IT'S YOUR OWN SPECIAL TIME
Contemporary romances for today's women.
Each month, six very special love stories will be yours
from SILHOUETTE.

$1.75 each

☐ 104 Vitek	☐ 131 Stanford	☐ 159 Tracy	☐ 186 Howard
☐ 105 Eden	☐ 132 Wisdom	☐ 160 Hampson	☐ 187 Scott
☐ 106 Dailey	☐ 133 Rowe	☐ 161 Trent	☐ 188 Cork
☐ 107 Bright	☐ 134 Charles	☐ 162 Ashby	☐ 189 Stephens
☐ 108 Hampson	☐ 135 Logan	☐ 163 Roberts	☐ 190 Hampson
☐ 109 Vernon	☐ 136 Hampson	☐ 164 Browning	☐ 191 Browning
☐ 110 Trent	☐ 137 Hunter	☐ 165 Young	☐ 192 John
☐ 111 South	☐ 138 Wilson	☐ 166 Wisdom	☐ 193 Trent
☐ 112 Stanford	☐ 139 Vitek	☐ 167 Hunter	☐ 194 Barry
☐ 113 Browning	☐ 140 Erskine	☐ 168 Carr	☐ 195 Dailey
☐ 114 Michaels	☐ 142 Browning	☐ 169 Scott	☐ 196 Hampson
☐ 115 John	☐ 143 Roberts	☐ 170 Ripy	☐ 197 Summers
☐ 116 Lindley	☐ 144 Goforth	☐ 171 Hill	☐ 198 Hunter
☐ 117 Scott	☐ 145 Hope	☐ 172 Browning	☐ 199 Roberts
☐ 118 Dailey	☐ 146 Michaels	☐ 173 Camp	☐ 200 Lloyd
☐ 119 Hampson	☐ 147 Hampson	☐ 174 Sinclair	☐ 201 Starr
☐ 120 Carroll	☐ 148 Cork	☐ 175 Jarrett	☐ 202 Hampson
☐ 121 Langan	☐ 149 Saunders	☐ 176 Vitek	☐ 203 Browning
☐ 122 Scofield	☐ 150 Major	☐ 177 Dailey	☐ 204 Carroll
☐ 123 Sinclair	☐ 151 Hampson	☐ 178 Hampson	☐ 205 Maxam
☐ 124 Beckman	☐ 152 Halston	☐ 179 Beckman	☐ 206 Manning
☐ 125 Bright	☐ 153 Dailey	☐ 180 Roberts	☐ 207 Windham
☐ 126 St. George	☐ 154 Beckman	☐ 181 Terrill	☐ 208 Halston
☐ 127 Roberts	☐ 155 Hampson	☐ 182 Clay	☐ 209 LaDame
☐ 128 Hampson	☐ 156 Sawyer	☐ 183 Stanley	☐ 210 Eden
☐ 129 Converse	☐ 157 Vitek	☐ 184 Hardy	☐ 211 Walters
☐ 130 Hardy	☐ 158 Reynolds	☐ 185 Hampson	☐ 212 Young

$1.95 each

☐ 213 Dailey	☐ 219 Cork	☐ 225 St. George	☐ 231 Dailey
☐ 214 Hampson	☐ 220 Hampson	☐ 226 Hampson	☐ 232 Hampson
☐ 215 Roberts	☐ 221 Browning	☐ 227 Beckman	☐ 233 Vernon
☐ 216 Saunders	☐ 222 Carroll	☐ 228 King	☐ 234 Smith
☐ 217 Vitek	☐ 223 Summers	☐ 229 Thornton	☐ 235 James
☐ 218 Hunter	☐ 224 Langan	☐ 230 Stevens	☐ 236 Maxam

Silhouette Romance

$1.95 each

- ☐ 237 Wilson
- ☐ 238 Cork
- ☐ 239 McKay
- ☐ 240 Hunter
- ☐ 241 Wisdom
- ☐ 242 Brooke
- ☐ 243 Saunders
- ☐ 244 Sinclair
- ☐ 245 Trent
- ☐ 246 Carroll
- ☐ 247 Halldorson
- ☐ 248 St. George
- ☐ 249 Scofield
- ☐ 250 Hampson
- ☐ 251 Wilson
- ☐ 252 Roberts
- ☐ 253 James
- ☐ 254 Palmer
- ☐ 255 Smith
- ☐ 256 Hampson
- ☐ 257 Hunter
- ☐ 258 Ashby
- ☐ 259 English
- ☐ 260 Martin
- ☐ 261 Saunders

- ☐ 262 John
- ☐ 263 Wilson
- ☐ 264 Vine
- ☐ 265 Adams
- ☐ 266 Trent
- ☐ 267 Chase
- ☐ 268 Hunter
- ☐ 269 Smith
- ☐ 270 Camp
- ☐ 271 Allison
- ☐ 272 Forrest
- ☐ 273 Beckman
- ☐ 274 Roberts
- ☐ 275 Browning
- ☐ 276 Vernon
- ☐ 277 Wilson
- ☐ 278 Hunter
- ☐ 279 Ashby
- ☐ 280 Roberts
- ☐ 281 Lovan
- ☐ 282 Halldorson
- ☐ 283 Payne
- ☐ 284 Young
- ☐ 285 Gray
- ☐ 286 Cork

- ☐ 287 Joyce
- ☐ 288 Smith
- ☐ 289 Saunders
- ☐ 290 Hunter
- ☐ 291 McKay
- ☐ 292 Browning
- ☐ 293 Morgan
- ☐ 294 Cockcroft
- ☐ 295 Vernon
- ☐ 296 Paige
- ☐ 297 Young
- ☐ 298 Hunter
- ☐ 299 Roberts
- ☐ 300 Stephens
- ☐ 301 Palmer
- ☐ 302 Smith
- ☐ 303 Langan
- ☐ 304 Cork
- ☐ 305 Browning
- ☐ 306 Gordon
- ☐ 307 Wildman
- ☐ 308 Young
- ☐ 309 Hardy
- ☐ 310 Hunter
- ☐ 311 Gray

- ☐ 312 Vernon
- ☐ 313 Rainville
- ☐ 314 Palmer
- ☐ 315 Smith
- ☐ 316 Macomber
- ☐ 317 Langan
- ☐ 318 Herrington
- ☐ 319 Lloyd
- ☐ 320 Brooke
- ☐ 321 Glenn
- ☐ 322 Hunter
- ☐ 323 Browning
- ☐ 324 Maxam
- ☐ 325 Smith
- ☐ 326 Lovan
- ☐ 327 James
- ☐ 328 Palmer
- ☐ 329 Broadrick
- ☐ 330 Ferrell
- ☐ 331 Michaels
- ☐ 332 McCarty
- ☐ 333 Page

SILHOUETTE BOOKS, Department SB/1

1230 Avenue of the Americas
New York, NY 10020

Please send me the books I have checked above. I am enclosing $_____
(please add 75¢ to cover postage and handling. NYS and NYC residents please
add appropriate sales tax). Send check or money order—no cash or C.O.D.'s
please. Allow six weeks for delivery.

NAME _____

ADDRESS _____

CITY _____ STATE/ZIP _____

Silhouette Romance